THE HIGHEST DREAM

Phyllis A. Whitney

When Lisa Somers became a tour guide at the United Nations she was following her desire to escape from the shadow of her father's fame, she thought, and find herself as an individual. Her new job would present her with enough problems, she didn't need to fall in love as well. But from the time Norman Bond "crashed" her tour, she found herself more interested than she wanted to be . . . Although aimed at a young adult audience, *The Highest Dream* is also sure to bring nostalgic pleasure to the older reader.

THE HIGHEST DREAM

Phyllis A. Whitney, 1903-

"Let us no more be true to boasted race or clan,
But to our highest dream, the brotherhood of man."

–THOMAS CURTIS CLARK

Curley Publishing, Inc.
South Yarmouth, Ma.

B-2

Library of Congress Cataloging-in-Publication Data

Whitney, Phyllis A., 1903–
    The highest dream / Phyllis A. Whitney.
        p.   cm.
    1. Large type books.   I. Title.
    PS3545.H8363H5   1991]
    813'.54—dc20
    ISBN 0–7927–1094–0 (lg. print)   91–13928
    ISBN 0–7927–1095–9 (pbk: lg. print)   CIP

Published in Large Print by arrangement with McIntosh & Otis Inc. in the United States, Canada, the U.K. and British Commonwealth.

Distributed in Great Britain, Ireland and the Commonwealth by CHIVERS LIBRARY SERVICES LIMITED, Bath BA1 3HB, England.

Printed in Great Britain

My thanks to ABE *and* SYLVIA BURACK
who suggested this book; and to
JANET, SUSAN *and* ELLEN BURACK,
who suggested three lively sisters

Acknowledgment

Grateful acknowledgment and thanks to those at the United Nations who made it possible for me to gather my material:

Mr. Carl Cannon, director of the Guide Service, and his assistant, Mrs. Lucille Samson; Mr. James Wang of the Question and Answer Desk; Mr. Irving H. Berenson, executive producer of the United Nations Radio Review; Miss Isabelle Silk, program assistant, television department, and Miss Trudy Glass of the radio department; Mrs. Elsa Linda Lindt, public relations officer for UNICEF; Mrs. Jeannette Fritsche, deputy executive director, U.S. Committee for UNICEF.

And with special thanks to the guides who always stood ready with information and friendly advice. In particular: Joy Casserly, Jacqueline Hubert, Kirki Sideri, Sallie Ann Fleming, Kailas Damania, Jane Miller, Mildred Robinson.

THE HIGHEST DREAM

1. Guided Tour

The taxi, following Forty-Second Street toward the east side of New York, paused for a red light, and Lisa Somers tried to peer ahead through the windshield. A hot summer breeze, blowing dust and grit through the windows, stirred brown bangs over her forehead and she patted at them absently.

Her interest in the scene ahead was real enough, yet when she spoke it was in an effort to distract her mother from an uncomfortable topic of conversation.

"Shouldn't the buildings be in sight by now, Mother?"

Mrs. Somers smiled, looking young in spite of graying hair. Her eyes were as blue as Lisa's, though her resemblance to her daughter ended there. Lisa looked a great deal more like her famous father.

"The buildings of the United Nations won't blow away before we get there," Mrs. Somers said. "Those big apartment buildings hide them from view. But as I was saying, Lisa, your father doesn't want to rush you into a decision. After all, you've another year to go in college. But it would mean a lot to him

1

if you were planning to come into his office at home in Washington. If only you could develop some interest in radio work from the news end."

Lisa settled back in the cab. Radio, radio! With her father a well-known commentator and writer on world affairs, she had grown up in an atmosphere of radio publicity that sometimes threatened to engulf her own life completely. She had no wish to hurt or disappoint her parents, but there ought to be some way in which she could have a life of her own that would have nothing to do with radio. If she didn't find the answer soon, the very momentum of her father's work would catch her up, bear her along on its furious current. Even her mother, usually so understanding, did not fully realize how she felt about this.

Mother had always made Dad's work her own. The needs of Dad's professional life ordered her existence. It didn't make sense to her that Lisa should feel what amounted to antagonism toward radio work.

"There's no need to hurry your thinking," Mrs. Somers said gently as Lisa didn't answer. "Look – you can see a bit of the Secretariat Building now."

Again Lisa leaned forward to look. A tall section of blue-green glass windows, metal-trimmed, rose before them thirty-nine stories

2

into the air. This was the building that looked a little odd when you glimpsed it from a distance, being so tall and seemingly thin. But Lisa had seen so many pictures of it that it was like a friend.

It was lucky for her that Mother had stepped in to help Dad by doing this UN errand for him at a time when he couldn't leave home. Reid Somers was working on a new book about the United Nations and he had needed special information that could be obtained only through personal interviews. Mother often helped out when she was needed; and since Lisa was on vacation, she had been able to come along.

When the cab turned north along a wide street, Mrs. Somers leaned forward to stop the driver.

"Here, if you please. We'd like to walk toward the entrance." The cab drew up to the curb, and Lisa stepped into a warm breeze while her mother paid the fare. Stretching to the left, below the great oblong of glass windows that was the Secretariat, was a low building with a dome rising in the center. The windowless, flat side of the building made a white backdrop for a curving line of staffs whose colorful flags whipped sharply in the wind. These, Lisa knew, were the flags of the Member nations, and beyond them, rising

3

higher than any other on this international ground, flew the blue flag, with its white emblem of world and olive wreath, that was the symbol of the United Nations.

Lisa drew a quick breath. No one could look at those flags without feeling a prickle of excitement. They stood for so many hopes of the world. It was good to see the flag of the United States of America flying in its alphabetical place, one with the others.

They walked on, looking up at the flags, holding on to their hats in the breeze. As they approached the visitors' entrance, Mrs. Somers glanced at the watch on her wrist.

"I mustn't be late for my first appointment. You won't mind my leaving you, Lisa? You'll be busy – there's so much to see on the tour. And we'll meet later and have dinner in town."

Lisa remembered a broadcast that her father had done months ago in which he'd told of the way the UN played host to the world with tours conducted by trained guides. He had made the tour sound so interesting that both Lisa and her younger brother Ted had wanted to take it ever since. But now Ted was away in camp, so the opportunity was hers.

They climbed the few steps at the visitors' entrance and crossed a great cement plaza that stretched to the bank of the East River. On

4

their left, set in the center of a widespread lawn, was the dramatic statue of a woman on horseback, silhouetted black against the summer sky. "A gift from Yugoslavia," Mrs. Somers said, "representing Peace." On the right, doors were set in an imposing façade of marble and glass that shone in the sunlight.

Inside, Lisa wanted to stop and look around at the cantilevered balconies, the great expanse of lobby, but her mother was moving toward the information desk. When Mrs. Somers had stated her business and procured her pass into restricted areas, she took Lisa to the ticket desk where the guided tours were arranged.

"You'll be in good hands here." She smiled at a uniformed girl behind the desk. "And I'll meet you in two hours or less downstairs in the public lobby."

She touched Lisa's arm lightly and walked away, trim and youthful in her navy shantung suit.

Lisa looked admiringly after her for a moment. Katherine Somers was headed for the offices of the great on a responsible errand, yet she looked as serene as if she were making a neighborhood call. Her "unruffled quality," Dad called it, and Lisa knew how much it meant to her father in his busy, hectic, far from unruffled life.

5

Lisa sighed and was not sure whether the sound was one of envy or relief. She often wished she was a less easily ruffled person. Yet sometimes she had the odd sensation of wanting to escape both her mother's calm and her father's all-too-public existence. But "escape" to what? She had no answer to that question.

One of the girls at the tour desk glanced at her and Lisa stepped up to pay her student's rate of fifty cents. A second girl stamped it with a number, gave her a small tin button for her lapel, which bore the words *Guided Tour*, and waved her toward benches where visitors were waiting to be taken through the buildings. Tours left every few minutes and hers would be called soon.

Lisa took a seat near a wall of glass windows that ended the lobby. Several people waited on nearby benches, but for the moment she paid no attention to them, lost in her own thoughts. Not that her problems were such serious ones. Perhaps that was part of the trouble. It would be satisfying to bite into something really tough and prove that she could handle it by herself, with no one to think for her and smooth her way.

Here she was moving comfortably through college, with a year to go and no future decided. She had a strong suspicion that when

6

she graduated, even if she didn't go into his office, her father would quietly pull strings, doors would open, and she'd find herself working at some job – probably in radio or television – a job that paid well and might be interesting, but which would have been settled without requiring her to lift a finger. Sometimes she wished she were more like her brother Ted. Ted, now in his first year in high school, already knew that the field of science was for him. No one would settle anything about his life except Ted himself.

A microphone clicked on and a girl's voice spoke through the lobby, breaking into her thoughts. "May I have your attention, please? Tour Seven is leaving from the glass doors. Please assemble at the glass doors. Tour Seven is leaving."

Lisa glanced at her ticket and saw the "7" stamped upon it. She joined the group of some fifteen people who gathered near the doors on one side of the lobby, all rather sheepishly avoiding one another's eyes. At the doors which read *Push* and *Poussez* they gave up their tickets and filed through into an empty corridor where two guides waited, one a Negro girl.

Following through at the end of the group, Lisa found herself near a girl of about her own age.

"Have you visited the UN before?" she asked. "This is my first trip."

The girl was plumpish, with straggly, straw-colored hair. She gave Lisa the quickly suspicious look of the city-bred, cautious about talking to a stranger. But Lisa's appearance must have reassured her, because she stopped chewing her gum and answered, "I gotta boy friend who works at the coat check desk downstairs. Lotsa times I come here on my day off." She shrugged. "It's a place to go. Ssh – she's gonna introduce the guide."

The little group shuffled its feet and waited, its attention focused on the two guides in their attractive light blue uniforms. Each had her last name and first initial embroidered on the left pocket of her suit in a darker blue, and around the left shoulder was coiled a decorative cord of dark blue, ending in silver tips. The guides wore no caps and their hair was neatly groomed.

The girl who addressed the group now had a faint accent and from the name on her pocket, Lisa guessed that she must be Greek. "I'd like to introduce your guide, Miss Judith Johnson. Please ask her anything you want to know. I hope you will enjoy your tour."

The pretty colored girl smiled at them and said, "Will you follow me, please?"

8

She turned down the corridor and led them to a glass-enclosed area where a plaster model of the United Nations buildings had been set up. With a pointer she indicated each of the three buildings – General Assembly, the one with the dome, where they had entered; the low Conference Building, where the council chambers were; and the tall office building, the Secretariat. Then, when she had explained about the gift of a check from John D. Rockefeller, Jr. to purchase this land, and had told them of a few other matters, she asked for questions. Everyone stared at the floor or the ceiling in self-conscious silence, so she said, "This way, please," and they all streamed into a long corridor that led toward the Secretariat.

The plumpish girl was still at Lisa's side. "Golly," she mourned, "I wish I could fit into clothes the way those guides do. Lookat the figure!"

It wasn't just that the guide's figure was trim; it was her posture too – the set of her shoulders and the way she held her head. There was no speck of lint on the blue suit, no trace of dust on her neat black pumps. She wore pearl button earrings and a white nylon blouse, and her black hair was set in a neat coil around the back of her head. She walked briskly and the tour hurried after her somewhat helter-skelter. Its members had begun to look at one another now, still doubtfully, but at least as if they belonged in the same group.

The plump girl had apparently decided to give Lisa a private tour. She pointed out the Peace Bell, sent by Japan, before Miss Johnson did, and later in the Secretariat lobby informed Lisa that the green marble was from Italy and the white outside from Vermont. Whenever she looked in the direction of the guide, her rapt expression betrayed wistful admiration. Here, if Lisa had ever seen it, was envy and heroine worship.

"I do believe you'd like to be a guide yourself," she said as they moved toward an escalator that would take them upstairs. The girl flushed and began to chew her gum rapidly. She stepped onto the moving stairway behind Lisa and looked up at the guide ahead of them.

"Sure! Who wouldn't? But can you see me squeezing into one of those uniforms? Or hear me talking like that? You gotta have a good education for this job. And you gotta be smart too. Wait'll you hear the speeches that girl'll give when we get to the council rooms. The guides know everything."

Lisa smiled. "I think you do very well yourself," she whispered. "You've been

10

giving me a sort of private tour right along. You've even told me some things the guide left out."

The girl brightened as they stepped off the escalator. "All tours are different. Some guides like to talk about one thing, some another. I've heard so many of 'em I can put 'em all together."

There was no more talking for a while as Miss Johnson opened a door and ushered them into the visitors' gallery of a handsome council chamber with rayon tapestry walls in blue and gold. Above the distant horseshoe-shaped table on the floor was a symbolic mural. There was no meeting taking place and Miss Johnson explained that the horseshoe table was used because it had no head; all who sat at such a table were equal. She pointed out the row of glass windows set halfway up the wide walls, behind which interpreters sat. On the arm of every seat was a pair of earphones with a dial. While a speech was being made on the floor, a turn of the dial enabled the listener to hear it translated into any one of the official languages – Chinese, English, French, Russian, and Spanish.

"You remember, this is the one place where the veto can be used," Miss Johnson went on, and then asked for questions.

Almost without thinking Lisa raised her

hand. "But isn't there a way now of getting around the veto?"

Miss Johnson smiled at her. It was a friendly smile that seemed to recognize her as an individual who had asked a good question. She explained that in the event of an armed threat to peace, an issue could be transfered to the General Assembly. Of course the Assembly could only recommend action, while the Security Council could order action.

There were one or two other questions and then they filed out of the room. On the way Lisa's blond friend glanced at her in awe.

"You know something – *you* could be a guide. How'd you ever think to ask that? You'd fit into the uniform too. And you're pretty enough." Her sigh was plainly wistful.

Lisa gave the girl a startled look. "Me – a guide? Why, I don't even live in New York City. My home's in Washington."

"If I was your size, and smart too, I'd move," the girl said impatiently and Lisa held back a chuckle. She almost envied an ability to yearn so much for a particular something – even when it was unattainable.

The tour went on, pausing before the long mural in the corridor outside the council rooms, then into the Trusteeship Council, and finally the Economic and Social Council. Here Lisa's attention quickened and she felt

12

especially at home. There was to be a great deal in her father's book about ECOSOC and all the good it had done around the world. This was perhaps one of the most thrilling phases of United Nations work. She could tell by the way the guide spoke that she too felt the same way.

"I wonder if you realize," Miss Johnson said, "that one-half the population of the world is hungry, diseased, cannot read or write, and earns less than two hundred dollars a year? If *you* were an average citizen of the world, you could expect to die before you were forty. You could expect to be ill at least half your life, and hungry a good part of the time."

She had their arrested attention now as she went on to speak about UNICEF, the Children's Fund.

"If all the glasses of milk the Fund has given to the children of the world were placed side by side, they would go around the earth five times," she said quietly.

Somehow the picture of those little glasses of milk marching five abreast around the earth to nourish hungry children was a moving one. The little group was suddenly hushed and Lisa could feel her throat constrict. This poised girl in the blue uniform had her heart in what she was doing, and because she felt so strongly, she had touched her listeners to emotion. As they followed her out of the room Lisa watched her more closely than before, wondering how it would feel to be in her place.

The great auditorium of the General Assembly came last, and Lisa slipped into a seat feeling as awed as though she had stepped into a cathedral. The dome of the room rose above them with its multitude of wooden battens arching overhead. Below was a platform and a pink marble desk where the Secretary-General and the President of the Assembly sat when a meeting was in session. High above the desk, a focus of the entire room, was the familiar emblem of blue and white – the crest of the United Nations.

This was a room to experience, as much as it was a room to see. There was a spirit here that came from ideas, rather than things. How satisfying it must be to take even the smallest part in all this represented.

Lisa was thoughtful when they filed out of the auditorium; she hardly heard the chatter of the blond girl, puffing along at her side. Had a window been opened on her own problem? Was this a scheme of things into which she might somehow fit?

The tour took elevators to the basement and there Miss Johnson thanked them and said good-bye. But when she started away, Lisa followed and spoke her name. The girl turned, waiting.

"Is – is it very difficult to become a guide?" Lisa asked.

Miss Johnson smiled. "I suppose it isn't altogether easy. There are a great many applicants. But it's not a career job, you know. They want us to stay not less than one year, or more than two, though perhaps it can be a stepping stone to something else."

"Maybe that's what I really want," Lisa said wonderingly. "A stepping stone. But if there are so many girls applying. . . ."

"Lots of them never make the grade because they lack the background," Miss Johnson said. "And of course only a limited number of American girls can be used – the guides must come from many countries. But if you have what is required, there's always a chance."

Lisa thanked her and went toward the stairs. She had forgotten her companion on the tour and when she looked around she saw her over at the checking desk, talking to a man behind the counter. The girl waved and Lisa waved back and started upstairs. Her watch told her that she still had nearly an hour before she must meet her mother. She thought of the Meditation Room, about which

15

the guide had told them during the tour. It was not visited by groups, but was always open to anyone who wanted a quiet place to think or pray.

Lisa climbed stairs banked with green plants and walked toward a bronze plaque set into the wall, honoring Count Bernadotte who had given his life in the United Nations cause. Nearby was the entrance to the Meditation Room.

She stepped into a curtained anteroom that carried a sign: SILENCE. Inside the small, beige-curtained enclosure were a few rows of simple wooden chairs. Only one other occupant, a young man, sat in the front row. The room had no formal altar, for this was a place for those of any faith. But where an altar would have been, stood a waist-high, polished section of tree trunk – two hundred and fifty years old, Miss Johnson had said. And upon it in a great brass bowl was a spreading green plant.

Lisa took a chair in the rear and the man in the front row did not look around. The green carpet was soft beneath her feet, the lighting gentle, and no faintest sound came from the outer world. She closed her eyes and tried to think about her problem.

This would be a startling step to take in her parents' eyes and she couldn't know whether

16

they would regard it as sensible or not. But the very fact that the work would take her away from home appealed to her. She had a feeling that she could never be anyone in her own right while in the shadow of her father. Equally strong was the feeling that this might be something satisfying to do.

When she pictured herself standing before a group of strangers as Judith Johnson had done today, telling them about the work of the United Nations, she felt an exhilaration go through her. She had always been self-conscious about speaking into a microphone, but she found a live audience rather fun to talk to. This would be a job to test the girl who took it. There was more to the work, she knew, than a by-rote recitation of facts.

Up front the young man moved and glanced briefly back at her. He was rather good-looking, with thick light-brown hair and gray eyes that seemed troubled and thoughtful. When he stood up and walked over to look more closely at the flourishing green plant, Lisa watched him curiously.

Again he glanced at her and this time he smiled in a friendly way.

"Did you know," he said, so softly that the hush of the room was scarcely broken, "that this plant is here in memory of someone who died in a war?"

"Thank you for telling me," Lisa whispered.

He smiled again and went out of the room, walking lightly. Who was he, and where did he come from? What were his problems? But Lisa forgot him quickly, thinking again of the decision she must make.

For a little while longer she sat in the silent room. Then she rose and went to find the office which employed the guides.

2. Popcorn Welcome

The Guide Service, Lisa learned, was part of the Department of Public Information, and its offices were downstairs off the public lobby. The girl in the outer office was friendly and Lisa explained that she was in New York for only a day or so. She didn't know when she would come here again from Washington and she would like to talk to someone about becoming a guide.

Mrs. Warren, the young woman who was the director's assistant, readily granted her an interview. She made it clear at once that the Guide Service had more applicants than it could use and that American girls were

18

very easy to find. Besides – wasn't she too young? A girl must be twenty before she could become a guide. Lisa explained that she had a year more to go in college in any event, by which time she would be old enough. If she could just be put on their waiting list. . . . No, she didn't know another language fluently enough to speak it. Was that an insurmountable handicap?

"We prefer girls who speak more than one language," Mrs. Warren said. "But when other advantages are important enough, we sometimes waive this."

She seemed to imply that in Lisa's case this would not be so. Lisa had the feeling that she was only one of many girls applying and that the others had better backgrounds for such work; they were girls who knew more languages, or had a political science education. Searching for something further that would make her seem exactly right for the job, she made another try.

"As Reid Somers's daughter I suppose I've been learning about international affairs since I was quite small. My father is writing a book about the United Nations now." She paused because of Mrs. Warren's exclamation.

"Reid Somers's daughter! Well, I should think you would have a background!"

Instantly Lisa wished the words unspoken.

She didn't want this job because of her father. She wanted it on her own, and because she deserved it solely and completely for herself. But the woman was smiling at her in a friendly way, rising to see her to the door.

"You're very persuasive, Miss Somers. And we like girls who can be enthusiastic. You have a good voice, too. And of course your background and home life – well, we'll see. Take the application blanks along. There will be a security investigation you know. Forms to be filled out and so on. Thank you for coming in. We'll let you know if anything opens up."

It wasn't final, but at least the possibility seemed promising. She left the office and returned to the public lobby, to find her mother, earlier than she had expected, looking into the lighted windows of a bookshop. Mrs. Somers turned with a bright smile as Lisa came toward her.

"My interviews went well," she said. "I was able to talk to Dr. Bunche himself. Your father will be proud of me. And how did you enjoy the tour?"

Lisa took a deep breath. "It may be that I have a job, Mother. For after college, that is. Not a – a career job. Just for a couple of years. But it could lead to something else."

"That sounds interesting," said her mother

20

calmly. "Tell me about it."

Lisa plunged ahead. "I – I'd like to work as a guide here at the UN. I took the tour and loved it. Our guide *cared* about what she was doing. She gave a thrilling talk about the Economic and Social Council. If I could do something like that –"

"Well, why not?" said her mother, her smile warming her eyes, lifting the corners of her mouth.

"Then – you think Dad wouldn't mind?"

"We'll have to see. You know we both want what is best for you. He has hoped, I'm sure, that you might be interested in some sort of radio work. But certainly work that would bring you into UN territory should please him. Of course we'll miss you at home. And there will be problems to solve. A good many problems."

That proved entirely correct. There were a hundred and one problems, even after her father had given his consent to this as something which would be a worthwhile experience, no matter what she did later on. Many of the problems came in printed forms with endless questions to answer, some easy, some baffling. Others concerned the problem of where she was to live, and with whom.

"I don't think you should be alone in New York," her mother said when it seemed

21

apparent in mid-December that the UN job was really going through. Lisa had suggested that she get a room in the city after she graduated, but both Dad and Mother agreed – no living alone in New York.

Reid Somers stood in the doorway of his study looking impressive and confident as he always did. He was a person with so much drive that most people seemed to swim along like jellyfish beside him. He could hardly be called handsome in the ordinary sense, but Lisa had never seen a man she thought more distinguished looking. His hair was still dark; he had a strong nose, and a mouth with deep lines in half moons about it. His dark eyes could fire with indignation or be entirely gentle, depending on the provocation. Now he was both firm and gentle. He knew a fellow in New York – a young chap with a wife and family –

"Katherine, do you remember that young couple, the Starlings, who lived down the hall from us when Lisa was about ten?"

Her mother remembered. "Bob was a car salesman. Rather happy-go-lucky. But his wife, Beth, had a serious head on her shoulders."

"The point is," Mr. Somers said, "that they live somewhere near the United Nations. I ran into Bob the last time I was in New

York. Suppose I write to him. He might know of someone Lisa could move in with."

Lisa remembered the Starlings vaguely and hoped they would be able to help. But they wrote that apartments in that area were quickly snapped up because of the vast personnel working in the Secretariat. However, something might arise by the time Lisa was ready to come. They would keep their eyes open.

Along with her college schedule Lisa managed to fit in extra reading that might help her in her work as a guide. She listened to the talk at home with more feeling of participation too. Her father's work on his book was now of personal concern to her.

In midsummer of the following year, with college behind her, the call came in a letter from the Guide Service. She would be able to join a class starting the last week in August. A date was given for her to report.

Bob Starling wrote, "Let her come! We'll put her up on the living-room sofa, if necessary, and keep an eye on her till she finds a place." But neither her mother nor father wanted her to accept such an arrangement. The Starlings had three young daughters and were surely crowded enough.

Then the break for which Lisa had been hoping came. Again it was Bob Starling who

23

wrote about it in his enthusiastic way. Beth had her hands too full for much letter writing just now, but usually put in a few words by way of postscript. There was a young woman across the hall on their own floor, Bob wrote, who had shared an apartment with another girl. The second girl had recently moved out and Margie Robbins was looking for someone to take her place. Bob had of course suggested Lisa and the whole thing was set. Lisa had only to put on her hat and come.

Lisa's mother remained quietly unimpressed by Bob's breezy way of putting things. She pointed out that this time there was no scribbled line from Beth, and she didn't quite trust Bob's judgment. But by now Lisa was desperate and willing to fight for what she wanted. When her mother said mildly that, after all, they did not know this Margie Robbins, and what if Lisa and she did not suit each other – Lisa jumped up and went to the desk for paper and pen.

"I'm going to write to Mr. Starling myself! I can't afford to be fussy at this time. The Starlings wouldn't suggest the girl if she wasn't all right. And besides, I can regard any arrangement as temporary. Once I'm there and get to know people, I can find another apartment, if this doesn't work out –

perhaps share one with some girl who works at the UN."

"Suppose we let her go ahead," her father said. "She's old enough to take the responsibility."

So Mother agreeably gave in; and Lisa wrote the letter and put it quickly in the mail.

Bob Starling had not told them what Margie Robbins did for a living, Mother pointed out, and was not altogether reassured when word came back that Margie worked in a department store selling cosmetics. How much would Lisa have in common with her roommate? Mother wondered. But Lisa said it didn't matter. She wasn't looking for a bosom friend, but a place to hang her hat.

Nevertheless, Lisa didn't quite believe she would make it until she actually found herself on a train pulling into Pennsylvania Station one Saturday evening late in August. There had been a tug of emotion at the final parting. Her mother wept a few quiet tears, while her father was pretty solemn. Lisa had not been immune to the emotional climate. She had a frightening feeling at the very end that she ought to cling to what was safe and sure. She knew she'd miss Mother and Dad and Ted terribly, once she was in New York. But Washington wasn't far away and

25

her mother said she'd be up for a visit before long.

It was Ted who sent her on her way more bravely by whispering, "Go ahead and show 'em. You can, you know," and she had hugged him affectionately for that.

In any event, here she was, and here was Penn Station. She was to be met at the information desk by the entire Starling family, and she inquired her way to it when she stepped off the train. But the enormous station spread away to right and left and the information desk in the center revealed no family of five waiting for her.

As she walked uncertainly toward the desk, a small, pretty woman in a flowered silk print, with huge, serious brown eyes and no hat on her brown hair, came toward her. Lisa remembered Beth Starling and smiled.

Beth's smile in return was brief; she looked distracted as she held out her hand.

"I thought you were Lisa Somers. You're the image of your father. Sorry my family couldn't come. Bob had to see a big customer unexpectedly tonight, and Mimi has a cold so I've put her to bed. She's the baby, you know – only five. I left Carol, who's eleven, home in charge. But Bunny can be a handful and I want to hurry back. Bunny's eight and I never know from one minute to the next what

26

she'll be up to. Of course it wouldn't be fair to bring one girl with me if they couldn't all come."

"It must be fun to have three daughters," Lisa said as they picked up her two suitcases and walked toward the cab stand together.

Beth rolled her brown eyes heavenward. "Sometimes I'm not so sure. But let's not talk about my family – you'll see enough of them if you stay in the building. Let's talk about you." She gave Lisa a quick, appraising glance and then lifted her finger to signal for a cab. "You'll look fine in a guide's uniform. Of course they care more about what's in a girl's head than what's on the outside. But most of the guides could make the Rockettes look to their laurels on appearance."

It was nice to be complimented, but Lisa placed no great importance on her average looks. She got into the cab first and Beth settled into the seat beside her.

"I'm glad it happened this way," Beth ran on a little breathlessly. "I couldn't bear to think of you being plopped in with Margie Robbins without a word of warning. Bob's always so optimistic. He's sure everything will work out and he's been holding me back from writing."

"I'm glad to be here under any

circumstances," Lisa said. "If there's anything wrong with Margie, I'm glad you didn't write my family about it."

"Oh, there's nothing wrong, really. But she may not be exactly your type. My girls like her fine. But you'll be the third roommate she's had since she moved in a year ago. She and the other two didn't suit each other and they left."

That was too bad, Lisa thought, undisturbed. She smoothed the black calf handbag on her lap – a going-away present from her parents – and glanced out at the buildings of New York slipping by in the late dusk. With daylight-saving time the evening was still light.

"Empire State Building on our right," Beth said automatically, but Lisa could see only the revolving doors at its base as the cab stopped on Thirty-fourth Street for the light.

"I'll do my best to fit in, whatever Margie's like," she said. "I'm so grateful to be here. And it is something for her to take me in sight unseen."

"Bob talked her into it." Beth made a little face. "He really is a good salesman to have done it in spite of her – well, I suppose you'd call them prejudices."

"Prejudices?" Lisa felt she had lost the thread of what this was all about.

28

"Oh, dear," Beth said. "I'm telling this all wrong. Let it go for now. You'll see what I mean." She leaned back in the seat, closed her eyes, and rubbed a finger along her forehead.

Lisa couldn't feel terribly alarmed about Margie, whatever her "prejudices." She liked most people and usually they liked her. Margie she could take in her stride, she felt sure.

"Any steady boy friend?" Beth asked, opening her eyes suddenly.

Lisa shook her head, amused. "I'm afraid not. I'm the wholesome type men like for a sister."

"Mm," said Beth, sounding unconvinced. "I imagine you have your chances. You're not exactly repulsive, you know."

Lisa laughed out loud. "Oh, I go out on dates, of course. I'm no man-hater. It's just that right now I'm more interested in other things."

Beth shook her head solemnly. "I was reading just the other day – oh, look! There's our apartment building."

Lisa was glad to have the subject changed. She bent to look out the cab window and saw the towering apartment which had cut off her view of the UN on that last trip here with her mother.

The cab turned into a driveway and came to a halt before a revolving door. A doorman in uniform touched his cap and stepped up to open the cab door. He piled Lisa's suitcases on the sidewalk and motioned the two women ahead of him into the lobby.

No sooner were they all inside than the glass doors went flying around again with a swooshing sound and a little girl of about eight, bearing two overflowing cartons of popcorn, catapulted into the lobby on their heels. She had her mother's great brown eyes, but not her prettiness. There were freckles on her stubby nose, a smear of butter around her mouth, and dribbles of popcorn like snow on the front of her red sweater.

"Mom!" she screamed, as though her mother had not noted her dramatic arrival. "I saw you in the cab and I yelled like anything, but you wouldn't look."

"Hello, Bunny," Beth said. "I'm looking now and you're smeary all over. This is Lisa Somers. Here, take my handkerchief."

Bunny juggled the cartons into one arm, took the handkerchief absently and made a little dab at her chin, wide brown eyes staring full at Lisa over the heaps of popcorn.

"How-do-you-do," she said as if a string had been pulled; then, having performed the amenities, she became herself again. "I'm going to be a guide when I grow up," she announced.

Lisa smiled. "That's fine. Then we can talk things over about this new job of mine."

The doorman, who had gone to the desk for Lisa's key, came back and picked up her suitcases. Beth led the way to the elevators in his wake.

"Why the popcorn, Bunny?" Beth asked. "I thought I told you to stay in the apartment till I got home."

"I know," Bunny said, tripping over the elevator sill as she followed the others in. "But this was a double desperate emergency. It's for Margie and Mimi's monster."

"You see what I mean?" Beth threw a despairing look at Lisa and the doorman grinned. "Tell me about the monster first. That's probably worse." She added to Lisa, "The monster is Mimi's imaginary playmate. Other children invent children for playmates. But not my child!"

"He lost a piece of his tail in the refrigerator," Bunny said tragically. "I asked Mimi where he was just to make sure. And she said he was under her bed singing a song. So I opened the refrigerator door to get a glass of milk and when I closed it she began to yell that his tail was in the kitchen and I'd caught it in the door. So if you find a piece of monster

31

tail mixed up in the ice cubes, that's why. The popcorn's to make him, and Mimi of course, feel better."

The doorman stopped the elevator at the fourteenth floor, choking back his laughter. He winked at Lisa as the others stepped out. "Great imagination, these Starling kids."

"Wait till you find the monster down in your lobby one of these days," Beth said bitterly. "You won't talk about imagination."

They stepped into a gray-blue hall, pleasantly carpeted in a darker blue, and Bunny went on with her story.

"There was what Daddy called a popcorn crisis with Margie's last roommate, remember, Mom? So Margie's getting set right away this time. She said she might as well know the worst about you, Lisa."

Lisa smiled. "I can take popcorn or leave it, so I don't think there'll be any trouble on that score."

"A fine homecoming for you!" Beth said. "A popcorn crisis! I'm sorry, Lisa, but –"

"Oh, I don't mind," Lisa assured her in amusement. "It's all so different from home and –"

"I can imagine," Beth said. "I remember your father very well. And your lovely mother. Never mind the bags, Stan, we'll take them the rest of the way ourselves."

32

The doorman gave them up reluctantly. Obviously he wanted to be in on this little drama. But Beth waited till he disappeared in the elevator before she picked up one suitcase, while Lisa took the other. Then she led the way around a turn into a hall that ran the width of the building. A second turn into a shorter arm revealed two doors facing each other across a hall.

Bunny ran ahead, popcorn in arms, and stood before one of the doors.

"Here's where you live, Lisa. Hurry up and unlock it and I'll take Margie her bagful. She said come right in and don't ring the bell."

Lisa set down her suitcase before she unlocked the door. Then she held out a hand to Bunny.

"Why not let me take in Margie's bag? Perhaps we'll do better if I go in by myself the first time."

"Of course!" Beth cried in relief. "Bunny, give Lisa the popcorn and come along with me. We'll see you tomorrow, Lisa."

Reluctantly, Bunny gave up the less brimming bag and followed her mother across the hall.

"Good night," Lisa said, "and thank you." She pushed open the door and stepped into the apartment, popcorn in one hand and a suitcase in the other.

3. *Margie Gets Things Straight*

Lisa pushed her two suitcases into the middle of a green and brown living room and looked about. There was no sound except for a whisper of curtains as a breeze blew into the room. The apartment seemed reasonably cool, in spite of the August day.

A lamp burned on an end table near the sofa and she saw that the room was definitely being lived in. A light-blue coat had been flung across one end of the sofa, a pleated skirt draped the back of a chair, and over the front of the radio cabinet hung a pair of nylon stockings. Lisa shrugged. She wasn't here to reform Margie. Though the state of this room showed no welcome for a newcomer who was to share the apartment.

"Anybody home?" she called, beginning to wonder if Margie had gone out somewhere while Bunny was getting popcorn.

A voice from another room answered readily. "Hi! Is that Lisa Somers? Come on in."

Lisa went through a tiny hall, off which a

bathroom opened, and crossed it to a bedroom door.

There were lights aplenty in this room – shining from the ceiling dome, from dressing-table lamps, from reading lamps over both twin beds, and from a floor lamp in a corner. In the center of one bed, bathed in this glow of light, was curled a girl with a blond swish of pony tail held back with pink ribbon. A girl who seemed no more than twelve, except that a twelve-year-old would have been less expert with lipstick and eyebrow pencil. Yet for all the careful make-up, Margie had a childish, wide-eyed look that reminded Lisa of blue pansies. She wore a pink shortie nightgown, with ruffled pink bloomers, and she was painting her toenails bright pink.

"I've brought you some popcorn," Lisa said, holding out the bag. "I met a special messenger on the way."

"Have some yourself," Margie said, watching her intently.

"Thanks," said Lisa. She took a handful of kernels and popped a few into her mouth. Then she set the bag against a pillow near Margie.

The girl on the bed eyed it with distaste. "I don't like popcorn much. It was just a matter of principle." With that enigmatic remark, she returned to the painting of a small toenail.

35

Lisa glanced toward the window and forgot Margie in sudden delight. She crossed the room to look out toward the east where the Secretariat Building, embroidered with sequins of light from within its windows and reflections from its surface, rose high and strong against river and sky. From here it looked so startlingly close that she felt as if she could reach out and touch it.

"What a wonderful view!" she cried.

Margie said, "That old hunk of building gets in the way so you can hardly see the river."

Their opinion as to what made a view seemed to differ. Lisa turned from the window and pulled the pin from her white straw hat.

"I'm grateful to you for taking me in, Margie. I was worried for fear I wouldn't find a place to stay in New York."

Margie rubbed a smear of polish off the side of a toe and shrugged. "I can't swing the rent alone. I was glad to find somebody so quickly. And Bob Starling sure thinks you're swell."

She looked up at Lisa, studying her again. Lisa felt that she was being measured, weighed in some way, but she wasn't at all sure what Margie was looking for. She managed a smile.

"It was pretty reckless of Bob to

recommend me. He hasn't seen me since I was ten years old."

Margie veiled pansy eyes and there was no telling what conclusion she had come to.

"The left-hand top drawer in the dresser is yours," she said, waving the polish brush. "And the middle drawer. You get the left side of the dressing table with its drawers. And the left hangers in the closet."

"Thank you," Lisa said. "I might as well start unpacking."

She returned to the living room for her suitcases. Coat, skirt and stockings hung casually where they had been tossed, and she wondered if she should pick them up. Would that offend Margie? Or would it just mean that she'd have the job of picking up after her roommate from then on?

While she was considering, Margie came into the room, walking on her heels to save the new coat of polish. Lisa decided against picking up and reached for a suitcase.

"We might as well get things straight right from the beginning," Margie said. "Are you going to fuss all the time about the way I do things? Are you going to boss me and try to make me over?"

For an instant Lisa was taken aback, but she returned Margie's look pleasantly. She didn't know what was troubling the girl, or why she should have a chip on her shoulder, but she did want to get off to a good start with her.

"I expect it's a good idea to get things straight. I certainly don't mean to boss you or make you over. This is your apartment, and you can do what you like in it. I'll take on my share of the work and the expenses, but what I'm really interested in lies over there." She nodded in the direction of the UN buildings.

"That's fine," Margie said.

She picked up one suitcase and marched back to the bedroom. Lisa followed her, carrying the other. Margie dropped her case and perched herself on the side of a bed.

"My home's in New Jersey," she volunteered. "But there's only my aunt there now. My dad died a couple of years ago and my mother when I was little." She paused and thought a minute. Then she added, "My aunt doesn't approve of me."

Lisa made a sound of sympathy, not knowing what to say to this sudden outburst. She unlocked a suitcase and began to unpack. Margie watched her for a while and then went on.

"Bob Starling told me about your father and all that. He told me about the way you're going to work as a guide at the UN. Do you really care about that stuff?"

"That stuff?" Lisa repeated, puzzled.

"You know – what happens in India, or China, or Timbuctoo. I mean – who cares?"

"I suppose I do," Lisa said.

Margie stared at her almost defiantly. "Well, what I care about most is Margie, and I don't care who knows it." Her tone challenged as if she expected Lisa to denounce her at once.

"Well, why not?" Lisa said, shaking out a skirt to free it from wrinkles. "How can we like other people unless we like ourselves?"

She was quoting a psychology teacher at school, and Margie looked both bewildered and unwillingly impressed.

"Bunny says you went to college," Margie told her suspiciously. "All the way through – with degrees."

"I've been lucky," Lisa admitted.

"Well, I haven't been," said Margie. "I couldn't take it with my aunt any more, so I came to New York and got a job before I finished high school."

"That's too bad," Lisa said gently.

"What's bad about it?" There was a sudden snap to Margie's tone. "Maybe you learn more things working on a job than they teach you in college."

"I expect that's true," Lisa went over to

39

Margie's bed and picked up the bag of popcorn, helping herself. "Different things anyway. And I'm sure what you learn in college isn't always practical. I'm a little worried about this guide job because I haven't done much that's practical. Have some popcorn."

Margie stared at her for a moment. Then she sat up and took a handful of white kernels herself. "Don't mind if I do," she said and smiled. When Margie smiled all the petulance left her face and she looked again like a cherubic child who had put on lipstick to pretend she was grown-up. Lisa sensed that a crisis had somehow been passed, though she was still in the dark as to its cause, or why Margie seemed more willing now to accept her.

By the time Lisa's things were unpacked and hung in the closet, or put away in drawers, the two girls were on more comfortable terms. Not exactly on common ground, perhaps, but at least on a workable basis. The first steps toward making friends with Margie had been taken.

The next morning, when Lisa crossed the hall to tap on the Starlings' door and Beth met her anxiously, she was able to report that all seemed to be under control and that she didn't expect to have any trouble living with

40

Margie Robbins. Even the nylons which still draped the radio didn't bother her, though she did not mention them to Beth.

Bob put down his Sunday paper and came to welcome her to New York. He was much as she remembered him – big and blond and good-looking. The happy-go-lucky manner of ten years ago hadn't changed and he was all the friendly extrovert.

"I knew you'd get along fine with Margie!" he boomed and only grinned good-naturedly when Beth pointed out that such an opinion had been pure wishful thinking.

Lisa was introduced to Carol, the oldest daughter, who was out in the kitchen washing breakfast dishes, while Bunny wiped. She too had Beth's big dark eyes, but Carol was far more serious than Bunny as she greeted Lisa. She was a slight girl who was doing her growing upward at the moment, instead of out. Her shy smile had a winning quality and there was intelligence in her dark eyes. She managed a quiet greeting, in spite of Bunny's excited juggling of plate and dish towel in an effort to get Lisa's attention.

Next Lisa must be taken into the girls' bedroom to meet Mimi, who was still in bed. Bunny abandoned her chores to Carol and came along, skipping and hopping and falling over her own feet.

41

"Quiet down, Bun-hon," said her father idly, and went back to his paper without noting whether his direction was obeyed.

Sighing, Beth went ahead into the bedroom and Bunny beamed impishly at Lisa. "He'll catch it from Mom later on," she confided. "She's trying to train him not to give us any orders he doesn't follow up. The books say it's very bad for parent-child relationships when you don't follow up directions."

"I can imagine," said Lisa, and went to stand beside Mimi's bed.

Obviously Mimi was the beauty of the family. She was the only one who was blond like Bob, but she too had her mother's big brown eyes, an altogether perfect mouth, and even the promise of good looks in her button of a nose. She showed her dimples in a wide smile for Lisa, not at all shy like her oldest sister.

"And how is the monster this morning?" Lisa asked. "I heard he had an accident yesterday."

Mimi flashed her a dazzling smile. "Oh, he's fine. He's like a lizard. He grew a new piece to his tail right away."

"Just the same he ought to keep it out of the kitchen," Bunny said.

Mimi wrinkled her button nose at her sister and turned her attention back to Lisa. "You

42

can't meet him now because he's gone to Sunday School. I gave him my pennies for the collection because I can't go today."

"And won't that surprise Miss Benson," Beth murmured wryly.

"Come and see my bird! Come and see my bird!" Bunny began to chant. Lisa told Mimi to get well fast, and followed Bunny into the living room.

"Thank goodness Carol likes books," Beth said. "Between Mimi's monster and Bunny's bird, things get a bit hectic around here."

Bunny opened the door of a cage which hung from a stand near the window and held out her forefinger. A gay little parakeet, heavenly blue with touches of yellow, hopped onto her finger. Bunny carried him over for Lisa's inspection.

"He's a budgie," Bunny said. "His name's Whirly. That's after the famous race horse, Whirlaway. On account of he is instead of a horse."

"She's at the horsey stage," Beth explained, "and we can't stable a horse in this apartment. The monster wouldn't stand for it. Don't touch that bird. He can bite viciously."

The bird was proving this by gnawing on the finger that held him, but Bunny seemed blissfully oblivious to pain.

"He's just mettlesome. He doesn't really

43

hurt," she added, wincing.

"When do you start your training class, Lisa?" Bob asked from his easy chair corner, rescuing Lisa from the bird.

"Tomorrow," Lisa said. "I'm anxious to begin."

She went back to Margie's apartment feeling that life might be lively indeed with the Starlings for neighbors.

In spite of her eagerness for tomorrow to come, it was good to have a day to catch her breath and get settled before she gave herself over to the absorbing work at the UN. That evening she and Margie went to a movie most companionably. Lisa let Margie pick the musical they saw, though there was a French picture in the neighborhood she would have preferred. The important thing was to get everything comfortably set with Margie. Then when her studies began she wouldn't have to worry lest Margie decide that she wouldn't do as a roommate.

4. School for Guides

The moment Lisa stepped into the lobby of the General Assembly Building on Monday morning, she heard the buzz of activity. Of course the G.A. would not be in session until the third Tuesday in September – the place would really be busy then. But even now there was more going on than there had been that midsummer day when she had been here with her mother the year before.

Lisa hurried downstairs and found two other girls waiting near the doors of the Tour Service office. They were chatting together in a mixture of French and English, discussing the matter of becoming guides, and Lisa couldn't help overhearing.

"Do you mind if I join you? I'm Lisa Somers," she said.

The pretty blonde introduced herself as Lizette Laverne, from Paris. The tall girl with the lovely complexion was Irene Stevens from England.

"I understand there'll be six of us in the class," Irene said. "A good group. We won't get so bored with each other before we're through."

The French girl laughed. "She means that we will listen to each other so many times when we give practice tours. Oh – I think here comes another for our class."

Lisa turned to see a tiny Chinese girl, in a pale-blue silk sheath with a high, embroidered collar, coming toward them. Lizette's smile drew her into their circle and she introduced herself as Jeanie Soong. A Spanish-looking girl who had stood a little apart, uncertain as to whether this was the class group, now joined them and said she was Carlotta Martinez from Ecuador.

The sixth and last girl was arresting, both because of her beauty and her brilliant costume. She wore a dark red sari which floated gracefully over a cream-colored robe. Her black hair was drawn into a knot at the nape of her neck, with a circlet of tiny roses about it. She had warm ivory skin and the fine features of the high-caste Hindu. The caste mark, a red dot, graced her forehead. She told them, speaking with a British accent, that her name was Asha Dyal.

Lisa found herself drawn to this quiet, reserved girl who moved with such grace and dignity. She was more curious about Asha than about any of the others.

As they waited, guides came and went. Would she ever, Lisa thought, wear their uniform with such casual confidence. Some of the guides glanced with open interest at the new girls, some smiled and spoke to them as they went by. One of those who spoke was Judith Johnson, the girl who had guided the tour Lisa took the year before. It was nice to know that she was still here — though of course she had seen so many people on tours since that time she probably wouldn't remember Lisa.

In a few moments Mrs. Warren, the same young woman who first interviewed Lisa, came out to greet them. She led the way to a basement conference room where their class would meet today. This was a smaller room than others Lisa had seen and was just right for committee use. Two adjacent walls were painted blue, the other two brown – an unusual and pleasing effect. A long polished table with curving edges and no right angles occupied the center of the room. The girls grouped themselves about Mrs. Warren at one end of the table and spread out their notebooks and pencils.

When Mrs. Warren was sure the girls had been introduced to one another, she began to speak about what the Guide Service stood for. It was organized after the move from Lake Success to the present site of the UN because there were so many requests from visitors to be shown about the buildings. Since its inception it had become one of the most popular as well as one of the most effective public relations projects of the UN.

"You have to remember," Mrs. Warren said, "that for thousands of people who come here, you guides are the only contact with

UN personnel. To them you represent the United Nations. If you do your job well these people carry the good word back to their communities. If you disappoint those who listen to you, or are indifferent to them, you can send them away with the wrong impression."

She went on to explain that the talks the guides gave were never memorized. Each girl must be so thoroughly grounded in her information that she could tell her story in her own words. During the two weeks of training they would be reading, listening, talking, absorbing information. Before they could give an actual tour, they must know a great deal more than could possibly be told in a single hour.

Lisa stole a glance at the other girls. Jeanie Soong sat absorbed. Asha, the Indian girl, listened politely but somewhat remotely, so that it was difficult to guess what she was thinking. The English girl, Irene, and Carlotta from Ecuador listened intently. As Mrs. Warren talked they all began to sense the responsibility that rested on the shoulders of a guide.

By now, Mrs. Warren told them, the number of the guides had increased from the original ten to many times that number. Among them they spoke over twenty languages fluently enough to be able to conduct tours in any major language required.

"Visitors from almost any country and from every state in the Union will be listening to you," she pointed out. "You will need to be aware of many points of view. You may talk to people from other countries who don't like the United States. You may talk to those from this country who don't like the UN, or who don't like the country you come from. Whatever the attitude, you must meet it with friendly courtesy. At one time or another almost anything may be asked when you call for questions. Most questions you'll be able to answer easily enough. But don't hesitate to say you don't know when that is the case. Don't try to bluff on your facts. It's quite possible that some of your listeners may know more than you do. There's a question-and-answer desk in the public lobby and you can refer to it any visitors who ask questions you can't answer. Then, when you get a chance, check up on the answer to whatever stumped you so you'll be ready for it next time."

Today, Mrs. Warren said, would be given mainly to orientation. They would go out in a little while and learn about the concourse basement, where the public lobby was located. There were three more basements under this one. In fact, the two low buildings of the group were mostly underground.

Time for study would be allowed during each day and there were private lounges for the guides in which this could be managed. They would need to read a good many books and pamphlets and could borrow some of these from the same question-and-answer desk she had mentioned. Every morning special briefings were held for the guides, to keep them posted on current issues, subjects to be discussed that day, or action taken the previous day.

Until lunchtime Mrs. Warren took them around, showing them lockers, washrooms, lounges; the post office which was the one place in the United States where UN stamps could be used; the large bookstore, where so many United Nations publications, both books and pamphlets, were sold; and the lower corridors that would take them into the restricted area of escalators and elevators in the Secretariat Building. They even had a brief look into the huge radio and television section where United Nations programs were recorded and broadcast. When in uniform or wearing a guide's arm band, Mrs. Warren said, they could go anywhere they liked. But visitors on tour were never supposed to stray away from the group and roam through restricted areas. A guide had to keep track of her flock at all times. That was why those little tin buttons were given out. They also prevented anyone who didn't belong from crashing the tours.

Once she mentioned shoes. "Better keep an extra pair or two in your lockers. You can expect to walk ten miles a day and a change of shoes will rest your feet."

By lunchtime Lisa felt that so much information had been pumped into her that it was practically oozing out of her ears. She was sure she'd not remember a third of it, and all the corridors and rooms ran together in a confusing maze so she couldn't remember where anything was. But she'd loved every minute of the morning and already she was burning with a missionary zeal to take out a group of visitors and sell them on the UN.

Just before they were dismissed for lunch, Mrs. Warren's voice pulled her out of that dream. "Of course we want you to tell people what you know and believe about the United Nations. You wouldn't be here taking this class if you yourself weren't already convinced of its importance. But remember – no preaching and no personal opinions. People come here on holiday, as a rule. They want to be interested and entertained. So no soap boxes are allowed. Tell them what you believe convincingly, but don't beat them over the head with it."

One of the older guides was going upstairs to the cafeteria and took the new girls with her. She led the way through the maze which already confused Lisa, and stepped onto the moving stairs.

The fourth floor cafeteria was not open to the public. Most of the employees of the three buildings ate here and Lisa lined up with the other girls, tray in hand. The food was good and inexpensive, and she, Jeanie, and Irene found a table near the big glass windows overlooking the river. Lisa glanced around for the Hindu girl, but she had disappeared.

The big bright room was crowded and as Lisa looked about she was conscious of the mixture of races, the multiplicity of tongues. There were blond Scandinavians, members of darker-skinned southern races, girls who might be from Burma, or perhaps the Philippines. One could hear French and Dutch, Chinese, Spanish, Russian, and of course always English, intermingling in the noisy chatter. It was not a quiet room, but there was something exciting about being a part of this lively mingling of people of many nations.

Jeanie Soong, small and dainty in her Chinese dress, smiled at her companions.

"We learn to know one another when we mix together. This is a good thing."

"I was thinking that too," Lisa agreed. "Too often Americans don't know enough about people from other countries. Our borders are so widespread."

Irene, glancing at a couple who were carrying trays toward an empty table nearby, said "Now *there's* an American. The man, I mean. I've learned from your films to pick them out of any crowd. They're good-looking – your American men – though in a different way from the English. It appears one of our guides is ahead of us, however."

Lisa followed her smiling look. A strikingly pretty girl with black curly hair and blue eyes that were matched by her guide's uniform, had just set her tray down on the table. The girl turned to make some laughing remark over her shoulder to the man Irene had noted. He was very tall, with light-brown hair. As he returned his companion's smile, Lisa wondered where she had seen him before. In Washington, perhaps?

"What nationality do you think the girl is?" Jeanie Soong asked, nibbling daintily at her salad.

Irene stirred cream and sugar judiciously, giving first attention to her tea. "In England we use hot milk. It seems unfortunate to cool one's tea with something icy. The girl? I should say she has an Irish look. Ten to one her name is O'Brien or Murphy. The hair and eyes are decidedly Irish. Attractive, isn't she?"

Jeanie regarded the tea operation in despair. "To spoil the flavor of good tea with sugar or milk is a sad thing."

Paying little attention to this side chatter, Lisa continued to watch the man at the nearby table. He must have sensed her interest, for once he glanced directly at her. She remembered him then and smiled in recognition. He was the man she saw in the Meditation Room more than a year ago when she first applied for a job as a guide. It was he who had told her about the green plant.

He seemed puzzled, though not unfriendly. Of course there was no reason for him to remember her. She was the one who had the most opportunity to observe him that day.

Now Irene was asking Jeanie about herself and Lisa listened with interest. Jeanie's father had been killed during the change of government in China. She and her mother escaped and came to relatives in this country. Jeanie's uncle was old-China and had seen to it that she attended not only American schools, but their own Chinese classes as well here in New York. Jeanie loved China and hated the

54

thought that she might never see it again.

As Lisa listened, she glanced now and then at the young American at the other table. She had a curious feeling that she knew him because of that brief exchange months before. But he was listening earnestly to the dark-haired girl and did not look Lisa's way again. The gaiety had left the girl's face and now there seemed something gently sad about her. Indeed, for a moment, she looked to be close to tears. Then, as the man said something obviously cheerful, she took out a handkerchief and smiled as she dabbed at her eyes.

"Come back to New York," Irene said to Lisa. "You're miles away. Ha'penny for your thoughts!"

"It's just my bump of curiosity," Lisa admitted. "I'm always trying to figure out things that are none of my business."

She did not look at those two again as Irene began to talk about the morning's training class. Certainly she didn't want to be caught staring. But later, down in the guides' lounge, she watched for the "Irish" girl to come in, still curious about her.

In the lounge she could feel herself truly a part of the tour operation. This was "back of the scenes." Girls sat about informally in comfortable chairs, several with their shoes off and sweaters substituting for their uniform jackets. Some read, others wrote letters, or ate sandwiches, or sat at the long dressing table combing their hair or freshening make-up. At the end of the room in a curtained recess were cots where the guides might rest if they felt like it.

Lisa saw an empty chair beside Asha Dyal and Judith Johnson and dropped into it. Today was fairly busy, so the girls had little time between tours. Every few minutes the telephone rang and the dispatch desk called for someone by name to come up and take the next tour. When a girl returned from a tour or from lunch, she phoned dispatch to report that she was back.

Lisa couldn't resist telling Judith that she had taken her tour and that it had decided her on this course.

Judith remembered her then. "I had a feeling at the time that we might be seeing you again. How nice that you made it. You've met Asha, of course?"

While they were talking, the lounge door opened. Several of the guides looked up as the girl Lisa had seen in the cafeteria came in. She seemed to be in more cheerful spirits now.

"How is Norman these days?" one of the older girls asked. Lisa was aware of fondness rather than banter in her tone.

The girl answered softly, and Lisa missed her words.

"Who is she?" she whispered to Judith.

"Oh, she's our special pet," Judith said readily. "Her name is Reland Munro and she's from Edinburgh – Scotch father and an Irish mother, I believe. She's been with us about six months and she's a darling. But homesick. She's finding it a bit hard to get used to America."

"Many of us must have that trouble," Asha said in her grave, quiet way. "We like many things about you Americans and about your country. But you also baffle us at times."

Judith's laughter was warm. "Funny – I don't feel a bit baffling to me. You'll have to tell us about these things, Asha."

But before Asha could continue, the phone rang and Judith was called upstairs for a tour. Reland Munro saw the empty chair and came over to take her place. She nodded in a friendly way to Asha and Lisa as she sat down.

"Hello. You two are of the new group, aren't you? It's nice to have you here. I'm fresh hatched from the fledgling state myself." There was more of the heather than the shamrock on her tongue and the trace was musical.

Lisa introduced the Hindu girl and when she mentioned her own name, Reland stared at her.

"Somers! So you are the one. Girls, we have a celebrity in our midst." Then she put a quick hand over her mouth and looked contritely at Lisa. "Perhaps now I shouldn't have blurted it out like that. Mrs. Warren told me only today and I think it's awfully exciting. Of course it's about your father I'm talking."

She smiled engagingly, yet with a touch of pleading in her look that seemed to say, "Don't be angry with me," and Lisa could only return her smile.

"What's this about whose father?" one of the other girls asked, looking around from her place at the mirror.

"Lisa Somers is Reid Somers's daughter," Reland said. "You know – *the* Reid Somers."

This time her words really had an effect and everyone looked with interest at Lisa. She could feel the unwanted flush rising in her cheeks. She had hoped that Mrs. Warren wouldn't tell anyone who her father was until it could seep around gradually and make no stir. But now Reland Munro had let the word out and there was no helping it.

"I have heard your father speak on the radio in Paris," Lizette said. "He is a most brilliant man. We think highly of him in France."

"Thank you," Lisa said helplessly.

"Last evening I heard his broadcast," Reland went on. "It gave me a warm feeling to hear the things he said about Great Britain. He can even criticize us without making us feel that he is in the slightest way prejudiced."

"This is true," Asha put in. "I have read his last book on the Asiatic problem. I believe he does not wholly understand the Indian viewpoint, but I feel in his writing a sincerity and liking for the peoples of the East."

Now the others began to question Lisa about her father, and when she said he was at work on a book about the United Nations, the girls were especially interested. There was no avoiding the spotlight Reland had unwittingly turned upon her, but Lisa had no desire to bask in it. This was the familiar pattern she wanted to escape. She'd have liked to talk to Asha further about India, but now it was time to return to class and there was no opportunity.

In the days that followed there was little time for personal discussion. The fledgling guides were caught up in classwork and study. The second of the two lounges where the guides gathered between tours had a long table with chairs about it. Here one could work, and Lisa and the others spent a good deal of time reading and discussing matters which came up in class.

Each day Mrs. Warren introduced them to a new council room. The day before they read all they could about it and then she took them into the room, pointing out matters of interest along the way. In the room itself she would touch on as many details as she could about the physical aspects, which always interested visitors. A lengthy discussion of the actual workings of the individual councils would follow – Trusteeship, then ECOSOC (as they learned to call the Economic and Social Council), the Security Council, and finally the General Assembly.

At home, when she had the apartment to herself, Lisa rehearsed her own version of the tour, with the furniture for audience. She would gesture grandly toward the windows, explaining the significance of a mural, or tap the radio with an umbrella, pointing out the buildings of the UN. She was especially clever when it came to answering questions, and neither sofa nor lamp was able to stump her. "Follow me, please," she would say and circle the room at a brisk pace, not looking behind to see if the chairs were keeping up with her.

Each day the class worked again through one building or another, retracing their steps over the tour. By the second week each girl was taking her turn at talking about these things to the others. Lisa felt awkward and self-conscious the first time, preferring an audience of sofa and chairs, but before long she relaxed and spoke more naturally.

Of their group Jeanie Soong did the warmest, most moving job. Asha was the brilliant one who knew all the answers and spoke the most carefully, yet one always felt her reserve. It was as if she could not quite let herself go on the level of her audience but remained intellectually superior.

"Don't instruct," Mrs. Warren would tell them all repeatedly. "You're not teachers on a higher plane. Just talk to us. Listen to the way Jeanie does it."

But Jeanie could pour out her heart. China was the homeland from which she and her family were exiled. As long as the world remained divided she could never see again its mountains and plains, its winding yellow rivers. So her yearning for peace found its way into her voice. The United Nations meant hope for the future to Jeanie, and she could put this feeling unself-consciously into words.

Now Lisa was so busy that for days on end she saw little of the Starlings, except when one of them looked in at the apartment to see how she was doing. Margie, noting how absorbed she was in her studies, offered to take on the meals for the time being. Lisa's background had given her little knowledge of cooking and she had to ask instructions for the simplest dish. A cookbook might just as well be written in Sanskrit, for all she understood of its terms. Mother could cook, but mostly she was busy playing secretary or assistant to Dad, and there was usually a hired cook in the kitchen at home.

"What does 'braise' mean?" Lisa would demand of Margie. "And why must they say 'sauté' when they really mean 'fry'?"

Margie, who proved surprisingly efficient in the kitchen, laughed and chased her back to her studies. She could read cookbooks later on, Margie said. Never mind now, or she'd be serving them Siamese on toast, or boiled Hungarian.

Eventually the nylons disappeared from the living room radio and Lisa wondered if Margie had been testing her in some childish way, challenging her to criticize. The girl still seemed to carry a chip on her shoulder, but Lisa had no time to figure out what it was.

After she washed the dishes at night, Lisa shut herself in the bedroom out of range of the radio and the voices of Margie's occasional visitors, and boned up on her studies. Only the persistent hum of Margie's electric clock intruded now and then to distract her.

Lisa thought she had a pretty fair grounding in her subject, and it was true that she was ahead of all but Asha in her knowledge. But as the second week moved along and the prospect of conducting a real tour approached, she began to feel that facts were water and her brain a sieve. She would stare suddenly at the great carved statue of a woman with a bluebird above her head on the wall of Trusteeship, and wonder what on earth it meant, who had carved it and why. Or she would freeze at the sight of the mural in Security and forget who had painted it.

It was some comfort that the other girls too seemed bright on one occasion and blank on the next. Mrs. Warren seemed to take it all in her stride.

"You'll be all right," she assured them. "Don't work at it so hard. By now you know more than you think you do, and it will be there when you need it."

Early one evening when Margie had gone out on an errand, Beth Starling came tapping on the door, a worried frown between her brows.

"Lisa, I know how busy you are, and I hate to make a request like this, but Bob and I have an engagement tonight that's important to him in his work. Our favorite baby sitter

63

has failed us. Do you suppose – I mean, if you could bring your books over and –"

Lisa could imagine what it would be like to study in the Starling apartment, but perhaps a rest from concentration might be a good thing.

"I'll be glad to come," she told Beth. "Just a minute till I get my key."

A moment later she returned to follow Beth across the hall.

5. Margie Arbitrates

There was a chorus of greetings and approval as Beth brought Lisa into the apartment and announced that she was to be "girl-sitter" for the evening. If it wasn't for the unpredictable Bunny, Beth whispered, Carol could manage Mimi by herself. But Bunny just had to be held in check by someone older. She had taken a liking to Lisa so everything should go well.

Bob Starling said, "Since our daughters are obviously angels, of course, all will be well."

His voice boomed cheerfully and Bunny, out in the kitchen working on a scrapbook said, "I'm not an angel, I'm a monster.

64

Yesterday a boy in school said so."

They all laughed and Bob and Beth, having kissed their daughters good night and admonished them to behave, hurried off. Lisa had brought along a book about the UN's Technical Assistance program, and she sat down to look through it.

Each of the three Starlings was happily occupied in her own way. Bunny was in the kitchen cutting out pictures of horses to paste in her scrapbook. Carol curled up on the sofa with a book. Mimi sat on the floor, contentedly talking to herself as she played with a tiny set of dolls in a cardboard dollhouse. Whirly, the budgie, was out of his cage, probably with Bunny, and no one had mentioned the monster. Lisa glanced at her watch. There was just time to catch her father's broadcast.

"Would you mind if I turned on the radio for a few minutes?" she asked Carol. Carol didn't mind and Lisa moved the dial to the right station. The announcer was just finishing his commercial.

"And now," he went on, "Reid Somers and fifteen minutes of what today's news means to the world we live in."

Her father had a good radio voice. It was distinctive, but without irritating inflections – a deep, quiet, confident voice. One felt instinctively that it was a voice of sanity in troubled times. Lisa listened to him every night that it was possible since leaving home and at first, in spite of her interest in her new life, she felt a twinge of homesickness. After a few days, that feeling died down a little. But tonight she was tired. She felt she had said some stupid things in class and that she wasn't going to be much good as a guide. The sound of her father's steady voice, so clear and close that it didn't seem possible he wasn't in the same room, brought unexpected tears. It would have been comforting to drop in on Dad and Mother and Ted for a few minutes and feel their encouragement and love. Her mother wrote often and her father when he could; there had even been a scrawled note from Ted. But letters weren't the same as being with the family. It was all very well to long for independence and an identity of her own, but Lisa still felt the strong emotional pull from home.

Her father was talking about the uneasy situation in the Far East and Lisa made herself focus on his words, instead of on the sound of his voice. There was talk of the United Nations stepping in and when the broadcast ended, Lisa turned off the radio to sit thinking about what he said.

Out in the kitchen Bunny hummed

contentedly to herself, Carol never once looked up from her book, and Mimi chattered to her dolls. Almost absently the notion came to Lisa that one of the dolls was talking back. A clear, but not quite human, voice issuing from the dollhouse seemed to be saying something that sounded like, "How-do-you-do, please-come-in, how-do-you-do, please-come-in," over and over.

Carol looked over the top of the book and regarded her small sister reproachfully. "Mimi," she said, her voice low, "you know you're not supposed to –"

But before she could finish Bunny came dashing out of the kitchen, her brown eyes dark with anger.

"You've got my Whirly in that old dollhouse again!" she stormed and made a dive for Mimi.

The youngest Starling slipped like a wriggling eel out of her sister's hands and crawled around the dollhouse to the other side. Bunny dropped to her knees, looked in one of the windows, and then stared wildly at Mimi.

"You know Mom said you weren't ever, ever to touch Whirly again. Last time you nearly choked him, and I'm glad he bit you."

Lisa, overcome by astonishment at this sudden turn of affairs, sat staring while Bunny dived again for Mimi. This time she made a capture and began rolling Mimi over and over on the carpet, pummeling her, while the littlest Starling fought back with teeth, nails, and kicking feet.

Lisa recovered herself and rushed at the combatants. "Stop it, girls!" she cried, trying vainly to pull them apart. But she might as well have directed the wind. A magazine stand trembled and went over on its side, and Lisa just caught the floor lamp in time. A tangle of waving legs and arms, tumbled locks, and shrieks of anguish marked the fracas on the floor. Carol merely watched helplessly, but without surprise. Lisa made another snatch at the broiling tangle and was kicked in the shins for her effort. At this crucial moment the doorbell rang and Carol, shouting that she would answer it, dashed into the hall.

A moment later Margie came into the room. "I heard the uproar from the hall," she said calmly. "Sounds like you're having trouble."

"Help me stop them!" Lisa cried frantically. "They'll kill each other, if we don't do something."

"Not those two," said Margie. "Much too tough."

She went to work expertly on the tangle,

unmindful of kicking feet. In spite of her size, Margie had strength. She got a firm hold on one arm and another leg and pulled the warriors apart. Mimi promptly burst into shrieks that were frightening to hear, while Bunny struggled to get to the attack again.

"Stop it, both of you," Margie said, and gave each a good shake. "Now then, let's arbitrate this."

"I want my mommy!" Mimi wailed and turned her back when Lisa went down on her knees and tried to offer comfort. But the word "arbitrate" caught Bunny's attention.

"What's that?" she demanded, pushing her wild hair out of her eyes and sucking at a welt on her hand caused by Mimi's sharp teeth.

"You each tell me your side and I'll be the impartial arbiter," Margie said. "Like in the unions. Then we'll come to a just decision and you'll both agree to abide by it. Come here, Mimi, and blow your nose." Margie offered a handkerchief with one hand and held out a stick of gum for each in the other.

Lisa dropped limply into a chair, feeling that the two warring nations were in unexpectedly good hands. Margie seemed to have an effective way with the young, and surprisingly enough the Starlings respected her.

"Now then," she was saying, having

staunched Mimi's flow of tears, "suppose you talk first, young lady. It looks like the fight is because Whirly is in your dollhouse. How'd he get there, anyway?"

Mimi hung her head and chewed gum vigorously.

"She took him!" Bunny accused, but the arbiter raised her hand sternly for silence.

"Mimi's not a baby," she said. "She can talk for herself."

Mimi flashed her a sudden smile and turned on dimples and charm. "I wasn't hurting that ole bird one bit. Whrily *likes* it in my dollhouse."

"Okay," Margie said to Bunny. "It's your turn."

"He does *not* like her dollhouse. It gives him kleptomania. He's all scrooched up in it and –"

"Not kleptomania," Carol corrected from her post of remote observer. "Claustrophobia."

"Don't be silly," Bunny said. "Claustrophobia is when you're scared by looking out a high window."

"Now, now," said Margie, "you're getting me all mixed up. You can play dictionary another time. You still haven't stated your case, Bunny."

"She's not supposed ever, ever to touch my
70

bird. Mom said so."

"That's right," Carol put in. "Mimi's too rough. She squeezes him. And besides, he belongs to Bunny and Mother says we're not supposed to take one another's belongings without permission from the owner."

"Seems to me," said Margie, "that the witness for the prosecution has just about sealed the case. Get your bird, Bunny. Whoops! Careful of those dolls. Now then – you two going to be friends?"

"Okay," said Bunny grudgingly. "But she'd better leave my Whirly alone."

Mimi, the warmhearted, could never hold a grudge. "Bunny, if you won't be mad at me, I'll loan you my monster to sleep with tonight," she offered.

Bunny, unappeased, returned to her scrapbook and horse pictures. Whirly perched interestedly on the paste pot and chirped, "How-do-you-please-come-in-how-do-you-please."

"The only thing to do," said Bunny in a voice loud enough to be heard by those in the living room, "is to achieve social self-sufficiency."

Margie grinned and dropped into Bob's favorite chair. "That gobbledygook her mother talks! It's a good thing I came along when I did. Why don't you go back to

71

our place, Lisa, where you can study in peace? I'll stay here till Beth and Bob get home."

Lisa was more than grateful. "Thanks a lot. If you're sure you don't mind?"

Margie shrugged and turned on the television – forbidden to the girls, except for certain programs. "What else have I got to do?"

As Lisa returned to the apartment she wondered a little about Margie. There were girl friends from the store with whom she went out occasionally, and she dated boys now and then. But mostly she seemed at loose ends – as if she marked time until something important happened. Since Lisa had grown up in a family that felt there was more to see and do and learn in the world right now than they would ever have time for, Margie's drifting attitude puzzled her.

Before she turned in that night, she switched off the bedroom light and stood beside the darkened window looking out toward the East River and the Secretariat, outlined against the sky. She was glad her life was so full of interest that there was no time for Margie's brand of idle waiting. There was so much promise in every day that she awoke eager for each new morning to begin. Her first day on actual tour was coming soon and she looked forward to it.

6. Gate Crashers

Having been fitted for her uniform, Lisa was disappointed to learn that it wouldn't be ready for several weeks. Just before the General Assembly opened, the guides would change from their light blue summer uniforms to dark blue. Then the trim would be reversed, with citation cord and name embroidery in light blue against the dark. The new girls would get their uniforms at the time of the change or shortly before. Now an arm band had to suffice. Jeanie and Asha would continue to wear their colorful national costumes, but the other new girls wore tailored dresses or suits.

This was Monday morning, the day of her first tour, and Lisa had been waiting anxiously to be called ever since she came in. All about her in the lounge the usual chatter ran on, but she heard little of it.

There was a briefing in the study lounge and the Chinese graduate student who conducted many of these briefings brought the guides up to date on what had happened recently and what might be expected to occur today. Several of the girls asked questions and there was a bit of discussion. But Lisa found it hard to concentrate. Her mind kept running helter-skelter over various details in an effort to make sure she knew what she was going to say on her first tour.

Only Asha and Jeanie seemed calm and confident.

"You remind me a little of my mother," Lisa told the Hindu girl. "Nothing ever seems to fluster you."

"Why should we be flustered?" Asha asked. "We know what it is we talk about. We have information – we give it."

"But what if they don't like us," Lisa murmured. "What if they don't choose to listen?"

Asha looked puzzled. "But they are here to listen. Always the American worries that someone does not like him. We can still do with poise what we must do. This is not a popularity contest."

But Lisa could not accept so cool an approach. With the girls from abroad she sometimes had the feeling that they spoke the same language only up to a certain point. She must try for a gathering of a few girls at the apartment soon. So far she had not mentioned it to Margie.

Now and then she glanced uneasily toward the phone. Every time it rang she jumped. Jeanie Soong had already taken a group out and was back in a state of quiet relief. All went well, she reported. The people on her tour had been interested and friendly. Their response was wonderful. Everything was going to be all right. Monday was Lizette's day off, so she wouldn't start until tomorrow. Asha had just gone out. So Irene, Lisa, and Carlotta waited.

Judith, coming in from her tour, said it was fairly busy today. She went to the phone to report that she was back and when she hung up she turned to Lisa with an encouraging smile.

"They want you upstairs. Don't worry – it's really easy when you get into the swing."

When Lisa stepped to the mirror for a last straightening up, as all the girls did before they went out, Reland Munro spoke to her. "A bit of bluff helps. I was terribly frightened the first time," she confessed. "But if nobody knows you're frightened, it doesn't matter."

This was good advice and Lisa stared at her reflection in the mirror with an air of confidence. A clothes brush on a chain hung from a hook beside the glass and she flicked a speck of two of lint from her blue suit. There was a list of reminders on a long poster near the door and Lisa glanced at it for the dozenth time.

The card was headed GROOMING and referred to hair, hands and nails, pointed out that make-up should be natural looking, listed permissible jewelry – no bracelets. Blouses must be tailored and freshly laundered – Lisa had an extra blouse hung in her locker. She had already given her shoes a last buffing with the aid of one of the shoe kits in the lounge. Now she checked her stocking seams, noted the emphatic word POSTURE at the bottom of the list, and went out the door with her head high and her shoulder blades back. If there was just some way she could straighten out the quiver in the pit of her stomach, she'd be fine.

A narrow, enclosed stairway down the corridor from the guides' lounge made a private short cut up to the tour section of the lobby. She hurried up the stairs and reported to the dispatch desk. The desk girls were busy on the phone, announcing tours, or checking records. One of them looked up at her matter-of-factly.

"You'll take Twelve, leaving in a few minutes."

"H-how many?" Lisa faltered.

The girl smiled at her. "About eighteen. I'm running some of this batch into the next tour so you won't be loaded with too many. Twenty-six is the top limit, but that's a handful."

Lisa sat down on the low, padded bench

along the wall and glanced with what she hoped was a casual air at the people who would make up her tour. Some of them were watching her with interest. Others talked among themselves, or stole sidelong looks at each other. There were some husband and wife couples, a number of singles, both men and women, and two or three children. All wore tour buttons conspicuously on their lapels. They didn't seem particularly alarming when she looked at them one by one.

A girl at the dispatch desk leaned toward her microphone. "Tour Number Twelve meeting at the glass doors across the lobby. Please assemble at the glass doors. Tour Number Twelve –"

There was a bustling as the members of the tour rose and crossed to the doors where a girl was posted to take their tickets. Lisa followed another girl from dispatch through a second door and waited beside her until the eighteen members of the tour were grouped about them expectantly. The men held their hats in their hands and one of them was smoking. On this mild September day the older women wore every type of costume imaginable, from fashionable fall suits to flowered prints and summer hats. The younger ones were bareheaded, and there was a pair of schoolgirls in socks and loafers.

The dispatch girl introduced Lisa, gave her arm a quick pat of encouragement, and went off. Lisa was on her own.

She smiled a little stiffly at the group, said, "Follow me, please," and led the way to the big model of the UN buildings, where she picked up the pointer and waited until they were gathered about the model. One by one she pointed out the three main buildings – the Conference Building, the General Assembly, the Secretariat. She indicated the little "neck" where they now stood, and with each flick of the pointer, her confidence grew. She knew this model inside out and she had no trouble explaining it to her listeners.

When she asked for questions there were none, and she explained that while smoking was permitted in many of the lobbies and corridors, it was not allowed in the carpeted areas they would now be visiting. She glanced at the man with the cigarette and was momentarily uneasy. He was a stocky fellow with a ruddy complexion and he looked like the sort who might be given to argument. But as she waited courteously, he tossed the cigarette into a container without objection.

Lisa set off again, the tour streaming after her. Now she was conscious of elation, of a spring to her step. She was over the first hurdle and beginning to enjoy herself. These were friendly, unalarming people and she meant to give them as interesting a tour as she could. If she was to represent the United Nations in their eyes, she'd see to it that they got a good impression.

At the Japanese pavilion, where the Peace Bell hung, someone asked if Japan was a member of the United Nations and she explained that a number of nations were still applying for membership. The Security Council must vote them in and so far there had not been the unanimous agreement necessary in that Council. When someone else wanted to start a discussion about why the applying nations ought to be allowed in, Lisa, with a mental eye on her time schedule, turned the discussion aside by explaining that there was a question-and-answer desk where they might go when the tour was over and where such matters could be taken up in more detail. The dispatch desk, she knew, allowed for a few minutes' variation one way or another, but a guide was supposed to keep within her sixty-minute allotment.

As she led the way toward the escalator she was aware of the intense regard of the two young girls and she gave them a friendly smile. Only the year before she had been in their place, watching a guide like herself with admiration and interest.

Her confidence was growing now and the last nervousness vanished. Now and then she caught glimpses of other tours. And in the council rooms there were always two or three separate groups with guides talking to them. The visitors' galleries were big enough so that they didn't interfere with each other. In Security she remembered to place her group one seat in from the wall, so that they wouldn't brush against the rayon tapestry wall-covering of blue and gold.

She could sense as she talked that most of the group was warming toward her. The only uncertain element was still the ruddy-faced man who continued to look suspicious and indifferent. She wondered why he had taken the tour if he was prepared only to disapprove of what he saw.

Everything continued well through Trusteeship, and she led her group toward the long mural in the corridor outside. This had been painted by the Spanish-Dominican artist, Zanetti, and depicted man's struggle for peace. The artist never gave an explanation of the meaning of the painting; he said it was for every man to find for himself. In class the guides had been given an interpretation and then allowed to add their own touches when they thought about it for themselves.

Lisa, leading the way to one end of the

80

mural to begin her discussion, saw two men coming along the corridor toward her. She realized they had to pass the group. She glanced at them to make sure there was room to pass and saw that the taller of the two was the young man she had seen in the Meditation Room and again in the cafeteria with Reland Munro. The smaller one – a slight, wiry fellow with an impudent smile – was observing her with frank interest.

As they came abreast of her group he whistled softly, but unmistakably. "Something new has been added," he said to his companion.

Lisa looked quickly away. She was doing well and no scoffers must throw her off now. From the corner of her eye she could see that the two men appeared to indulge in a slight disagreement. Then, obviously at the smaller one's insistence, they paused near the windows opposite the mural, leaning on a balcony rail, watching her, waiting to hear what she was going to say.

For the first time she felt slightly flustered, but she began her story about the mural resolutely and tried not to see the delighted grin the impudent young man was wearing. Nevertheless, she wondered if something was the matter. Was she as funny as all that? Or as simple-minded? Her listeners seemed to be following her; only one or two looked bored and restless, but the girls had said that it was sometimes hard to hold a group at the mural.

She was relieved when her talk about the picture came to an end. Now she could be on her way to the General Assembly, leaving the two mocking observers behind.

She walked at the good pace the guides adopted to keep the tours from lingering too long on the way, and took them into the General Assembly. She went down the steps to the rail of the visitors' gallery and seated her tour in a compact group. The two unwanted young men had attached themselves to her group and had followed the others in. Before she could intervene, they filed into seats right along the rest, watching her expectantly. Reland's friend seemed interested and attentive, while the other was mainly amused.

The young men wore no buttons and of course did not belong on the tour. Probably she ought to ask them to leave. But she had the feeling that the one with the impudent smile might react in some difficult way if she objected to their presence. So far no one in the tour seemed to be aware that newcomers had attached themselves, so perhaps the best thing to do was to ignore them and go ahead as if they weren't there. But she wished this hadn't happened on her very first tour.

Her lips had gone a little dry and she touched them with her tongue as she went carefully into her talk about the General Assembly.

"This room has been made to look smaller than it is," she told her audience. "That is so those meeting here can have some feeling of intimacy about working together. It is, however, the same size as Radio City Music Hall, and you know how big that is. The large abstract murals on each side are intended to draw the room together. And so do the overhead battens, which are for acoustical purposes."

She turned to glance at the scene behind her and pick up details to talk about. She wanted to tell them about the pink marble desk where the president of the Assembly and the Secretary-General would sit when the Assembly was in session. But even as she glanced toward the front of the room a dreadful realization struck her. She had completely skipped ECOSOC! The Economic and Social Council was one of the most interesting to talk about, perhaps the most important for visitors to hear about. But in her anxiety to get away from the eyes of those two young men, she had led her tour right by the door and forgotten it. Now she would be through too soon and she would have skipped an entire council room.

Even as her voice went obediently on talking about the desk, and about the rows of long tables below where the delegates' seats were arranged alphabetically, her mind considered possibilities. This room was the last stop, with the elevators nearby to return the tour to the basement. She couldn't march them all back over the same route to the Conference Building and then double back here. It would be too obvious that something was wrong. Nor could she think of any good excuse to offer.

Again she was aware of the exaggerated expression of attention upon the impudent face of the short man in the back row, and the impersonal interest of his companion. Suddenly she went jittery. She couldn't confess that she'd forgotten ECOSOC. She would have to skip it and hope for the best.

With her confidence so suddenly evaporated, she knew she was beginning to sound wooden, was reciting by rote – which was the very thing guides were never supposed to do. Until this moment most of the group had seemed interested in everything she had told them, but now there were some restless glances about the room and she could feel that her audience had ceased to attend to what she was saying. She got through somehow, her hands clammy. All she wanted now was to get the job done and escape. She hoped there would be few questions. But when she gave them a chance, the ruddy-faced man who had seemed the one antagonistic point of focus in the tour all along, pinned her with his pale gaze and said, "Who pays for all this?"

She knew the answers perfectly well. She had given them a dozen times in class. She knew that this was a question every guide was likely to be asked. She had been warned that she must regard no questioner as antagonistic; that she must answer even the most challenging question moderately and courteously. But now, her mind went blank. Every figure she had ever known left her.

"The – the nations all share in the – upkeep," she faltered and knew that she sounded uncertain.

"Yeah, I know," the man said, looking as if he were beginning to enjoy himself for the first time. "But how much of the bill do *we* have to pick up?"

Lisa sparred for time. "Whom do you mean by 'we'?"

"The USA, of course. We're supporting all this, aren't we? Just like we're trying to support the world."

The rest of the tour squirmed in discomfort.

Several turned to look indignantly at the speaker. Others merely watched the guide, waiting to see what she would answer. At least they were no longer bored.

Indignation flooded through Lisa in a sudden current. She was angry with those two in the back row who had thrown her out of stride and angry with the man who was baiting her, and who thought he had trapped her. But with the reasoning part of her mind she knew that the one thing she must never show while in charge of a tour was anger. She took a deep breath and managed a smile for her challenger. Her mind was quite clear now.

"A recent UN budget for one year was forty-one million dollars, of which the United States paid one-third. That amounts to about eight and one-half cents per person, or about what it costs New York city for its street cleaning bill in the course of a year. Four other countries pay more per capita than we do – Canada, Sweden, Iceland, and New Zealand. The amount paid is based on factors like world trade, dollar availability, and damage suffered by a country in the last war. Anyway, don't you think it's a pretty small sum to pay toward the peace of the world?"

The red-faced man wriggled in his seat. "I don't see peace anywhere in the world."

"And we won't see it while there is so

much poverty," Lisa said quickly. "The former Secretary-General, Trygve Lie, says in his book that poverty is the chief enemy of mankind. That's the enemy the UN is fighting. Now – are there any more questions?"

Someone wanted to know where the interpreters sat, and Lisa was able to get onto safer ground. Someone else asked who occupied the chairs that stretched diagonally on each side of the platform and she explained about distinguished visitors. She gave them full time with their questions, since she had cut the tour shorter than she had intended. When the group was finally silent, she led the way to the elevators, carefully ignoring the two men in the last row.

She wasn't frightened or self-conscious now; she was simply indignant with herself. When her tour reassembled in the public lobby in the basement, she indicated points of interest there, thanked them for taking the tour, and said good-by. One woman spoke up to thank her and several others murmured appreciative words. But she couldn't respond as warmly as she'd have liked to because of the conviction that she had done a poor job on her very first tour.

When the members of the tour wandered off in various directions, she turned toward the lounge to check with dispatch and see whether she was supposed to go to lunch now. The two young men had not been with the group in the basement, but now she saw them standing off to one side, still watching her. As she turned away, the shorter one came toward her.

"Good for you," he said with cheery impudence. "I liked the way you told old red-ears off. You're a little green still, but you'll improve with practice."

The other man stayed back and she thought he looked uncomfortable. Now that she was no longer in charge of a tour she had no hesitation about facing these two.

"Thank you," she told the impudent young man. "That was my first tour. I'm glad to know that I can hope to improve."

She caught the quick look the other man gave her, and for the first time he spoke to her directly. "Your first tour? And we spoiled it for you!" He looked both sorry and kind, but she had to place the blame where it belonged.

"I spoiled it for myself," she said. "If I can't deal with whatever comes up unexpectedly then I'm not much good at this."

She would have turned away then, but the short man stopped her.

"Look," he said, "we'd like to make it

up to you. I'm Jimmy Webb and this is Norman Bond. How about letting us take you to lunch? We owe you that much – to show we're sorry."

But this wasn't something she wanted to accept.

"No, thank you," she said quietly and went off toward the lounge.

7. *Lost Tour*

Lisa found she wasn't very hungry. She took a light salad on her tray and a roll, then moved along the counter to pick up a glass of milk. The cafeteria was fairly crowded as usual, but as she paused at the cashier's desk, she saw a couple of girls getting ready to leave a table near the window overlooking the East River. There were other guides at tables around the room – their uniforms stood out conspicuously. But she avoided their eyes in order to be alone for a little while. She wasn't ready to meet questions about how she had done on her first tour.

At the small table she unloaded her tray and sat down. Her throat still felt dry – from nervousness, more than from speaking – and

89

she took a swallow of cold milk.

"Would you mind if I sat here?" said a voice at her elbow.

She looked up startled to see Norman Bond standing beside her.

"I won't blame you if you snap at me," he said, "but I'd like to talk to you. I really am sorry, you know. That was a smart-alecky trick to play."

He sounded so contrite that she had to forgive him. His own lunch was considerably heartier than hers and he spread it out at the opposite place and slid his long length into a chair.

"I'd like you to believe," he went on, spooning sugar into his coffee, "that I don't always go along with Jimmy's playful tricks. I suppose this sounds like an old gag, but there was something about you that I couldn't quite place, and I wanted to follow along until it clicked. I have the feeling that I've met you somewhere."

So he remembered too, even though he hadn't placed her yet. She wondered if he would recall the meeting.

"I appear to resemble a lot of people," she said lightly.

He was still puzzled, but he let the matter go for the moment. "What I really wanted to say, if you don't mind, is that I think you were doing a good job this morning. If you got off your stride for a few minutes, that was our fault. You recovered neatly enough; you needn't worry."

"You don't know what I did!" Lisa put down her forkful of cottage cheese. "I skipped the Economic and Social Council entirely. I simply forgot it existed!"

Norman Bond began to laugh. But there was no ridicule in his laughter – this was simply a good joke. And suddenly she too saw it as a joke and laughed with him.

"After all," she said, really amused now, "that was my first tour, not my last."

"You'll go out and knock 'em dead this afternoon," he encouraged. "And another thing – I thought it was swell the way you took the blame yourself downstairs just now when we spoke to you. Some girls would have lit into Jimmy and blamed him."

She was pleased by his praise, but she tried to disparage what she had done. "After all, it's true. It *was* my fault. I shouldn't have been thrown out of stride so easily."

"Just the same –" he began and then glanced up as Reland Munro stopped by their table.

She was carrying a tray and Norman got to his feet at once, pulling out a chair. "Join us, Reland. There's lots of room."

The other girl hesitated, glancing at Lisa.

"Please do," Lisa said quickly.

Reland smiled and put down her tray. Norman helped her to unload it and stacked it on others at a nearby table.

"I've been apologizing," he explained, returning to his meal. "Jimmy and I crashed a first tour this morning, and I'm afraid we were a bit upsetting."

Reland shook her head sympathetically at Lisa. "How dreadful! Jimmy's such a tease – it probably looked like good fun to him at the time. But he's nice, really. He'd never intend to be mean, I can promise."

"It's all over now," Lisa said. She glanced at her watch, then began to eat more hurriedly.

"Better not start bolting your meals," Norman warned. "Reland used to do that. You guides work at high pressure a good part of the time, so you need to slow down in between."

Reland's smile was gentle. "I don't know what I'd have done without Norman to play counselor. He's perfectly right, but your first day is sure to be hard. Do you think you'e going to like the work, Lisa?"

"I already do," Lisa said. But she was curious about Norman Bond. "You're in the radio department, aren't you?" she asked him. "What sort of work do you do?"

"Oh – I'm a sort of odd job boy," he admitted. "I do announcing on minor occasions, help a bit with script production – that sort of thing."

"He's done some splendid interviews," Reland said. "He has a way of getting the person he's talking to, to relax and sound natural on the air."

There was liking in the way Norman looked at Reland. "It's hard to be modest around here. But just for the record – I interview only lesser lights and not many of them. I've been around nearly a year, but I'm still breaking in."

"What does Jimmy do?" Lisa asked.

"He's an engineer. And a pretty good one. I really got into the department through him. He's from my home town in Connecticut and he knew I played around with radio a bit when I was in the army in Germany. And that I was pretty interested in the UN. So he introduced me to some people, and here I am. Jimmy and I share living quarters now on the East Side. And that makes it your turn, Lisa. First – the rest of your name, please, then your history."

He was smiling, but Lisa glanced hastily at her watch. "I'm sorry. The rest of my name is Somers. But I'll have to get back soon, and there isn't much history. I took the tour one day and fell for the uniform. That's about all."

"Of course," Norman said. "The Guide Service always picks girls with frivolous intentions. But we'll postpone this for the next interview. Just so I can be sure we're forgiven – Jimmy and I."

Lisa nodded. "Of course you are."

"That's fine." He stood up as she rose to leave, and Reland smiled at her. "See you later," she said.

Lisa went out to the escalators and rode down to the basement to report in from lunch. She found herself wondering a little about Norman and Reland. Obviously there was a strong friendship between them, but there was no telling if it was anything more. Of course it was none of her business, but she was always interested in people.

Before long she was called for her second tour and this time she was only a little nervous to start with. She told her stories well and was able to answer most of the questions asked her. She even managed to remember ECOSOC.

When she returned to the lounge she no longer hesitated about telling the other girls what had happened on her first tour. Now she could turn the joke lightly on herself. When she mentioned Jimmy Webb, Judith laughed.

"It would be! Jimmy collects guides. In fact, he collects girls."

"I'm surprised at Norman Bond," another girl said. "Wish he'd look my way. But Reland has an inside track. And since we all love Reland –" she shrugged and a ripple of laughter ran around the room.

Lisa, however, had no time for side distractions the rest of that day. Her job was too absorbing and challenging. At closing time, in spite of her weariness, she decided to treat herself to something from the UN gift shop, by way of celebration over a successful first day.

She stood at the counter in the alcove where craft work from many nations was sold and looked at a cluster of pottery pig banks from Mexico. They were plump little fellows, with fat sides that could accommodate a good many pennies. Their tails curled over their backs to make a handle by which they could be lifted, and each had been individually hand-painted. Flowers of lavender and blue and green decorated their gray clay bodies and their painted faces wore a variety of expressions. Lisa picked one with a green snout, protruding green ears and a wistful look in its eyes. The price was small and she bought an extra one to send to Ted.

When Lisa took the pig bank home, Margie fell in love with it and made a ceremony of dropping four pennies through the slit in his side – to get "Pedro" off to a good start. After dinner the three young Starlings popped in to hear how Lisa's first day as a guide had gone. Bunny brought her bird and Mimi brought the monster.

Margie, as Lisa had observed, was surprisingly good with children, and both Mimi and Bunny seemed to adore her. Carol was more dreamy and aloof and it wasn't always possible to guess what she was thinking.

"Goodness!" Margie cried, staring at the floor at Mimi's feet. "He's cold, isn't he, the poor monster? All his three thousand teeth are chattering. I tell you what – I'll take him into the bathroom where it's nice and warm and he can stop shivering."

Bunny shook her head. "He won't fit in the bathroom. When he's stretched out in the hall he reaches clear to the elevators."

"Oh, yes, he will," said Margie, her blond pony tail bouncing in emphasis. "He can wind himself right around the radiator – like thread on a spool – and he'll be happy there until you're ready to go."

Mimi and Margie went off together and Bunny held Whirly up against her cheek where he gave her a little kiss. He was a cuddly bird when he wasn't chewing on a finger.

"At least we won't have the old thing under our feet and breathing down our necks," Bunny said, referring to the monster.

Carol regarded her sister despairingly. "Honestly, Bunny, you're as bad as Mimi. How is she ever going to grow up if you keep encouraging her?"

When Mimi and Margie came back, Lisa had to give another account of her day and tell them about the funny thing she had done that morning. The only point she left out was the fact that she had seen one of the tour-crashers later on at lunch time. She suspected that both Bunny and Margie would have seized upon that with interest.

When Beth summoned the girls home, Whirly said, "How-do-you-do," politely, and after first unwinding the monster, they all went home. Lisa kicked off her shoes and headed for the bedroom as soon as they were gone. She hadn't taken out as many tours as the more experienced girls did in one day, but she was weary from head to toe. Limp but happy, she flopped down on the bed. It wasn't just the walking, though she knew now why the girls kept extra pairs of shoes in their lockers. The work was tiring in another way too. She poured herself out to such a degree in the talks she gave and was so stimulated by her contacts with the public, that she was emotionally drained.

Gradually, as the days went by, she learned not to use up her energy so prodigally as she had that first day. As she became less tense, her ability to do a relaxed job increased and she was not so tired by night. She looked forward to her tours now and became more interested in the people she took out and the response she evoked in them.

Now and then she saw Norman and Jimmy together in the cafeteria and exchanged "hellos" with them. Sometimes she saw Norman lunching with Reland, or walking outside with her along the promenade on the river front. Apparently it was as the other girls had said, and there was more than friendship between these two.

Then one day Lisa had an unexpected talk with Reland alone. When the day was bright, she often sat outside at noontime on one of the benches that lined the wide cement walk above the river. This area was open only to UN personnel, so no one saw the badge on her arm and dashed up to ask directions.

It was pleasant to sit in the September sunshine, watching gulls soar above the little islands out in the river, and listening to the lap of waves against the wall far below. The walk was built above the East Side highway and the purring swish of unseen cars was a constant part of the outdoor sounds. Buoy bells clanged on the water and craft of various sizes glided by.

This noon hour Lisa was leaning on the wall watching the gulls dart and glide close to the water, when Reland Munro stopped beside her.

"They're rather fun to watch, don't you think?" Reland said. "They remind me of holidays in the Hebrides."

While Reland always spoke to her in passing, this was the first time they were alone. Lisa found herself thinking again how strikingly pretty this girl from Edinburgh was, and how engagingly gentle in manner. She wondered how Reland could manage to conduct a tour in so soft and gentle a way. Perhaps everyone liked her so readily that there was an instinctive desire to please and assist her.

"The Hebrides," Lisa echoed. "How wonderful to have been there. That's one of the names I used to say aloud to myself when I was little. I loved to chant names like Shanghai and Rangoon and Aberdeen."

"And Minneapolis, Minnesota," Reland

said. "Now there's a name to roll on the tongue!"

They laughed together in friendly understanding.

"Just the same," said Reland, "they make me a little homesick. The gulls, I mean."

She leaned toward the river, as if to watch the sightseeing boat that was passing, but Lisa caught the sadness in her voice and saw that she was blinking.

"Are you getting used to New York?" Lisa asked, trying to sound matter-of-fact.

"Oh, I love New York." Reland followed the boat with her eyes as it went toward the great span of the Queensboro Bridge. "There's so much to see and do. Edinburgh seems quiet beside it. Though of course that's where my heart belongs."

"Will you go home when you've finished your work here as a guide?"

Reland hesitated. "I'll not be going home for quite a long while." She turned then and smiled at Lisa. "What of yourself? Where do you go from here, when you're through with the guide service?"

"I don't know yet," Lisa said. "I haven't really thought about it."

"Norman's been asking me how you are doing," Reland went on.

"Fine, I hope," Lisa said. "At least I

haven't pulled any more really big boners."

"I'll tell him that," said Reland. "He was terribly interested to hear that you are Reid Somers's daughter. He has admired your father for a long time. I know Norman had a feeling all along that he had seen you somewhere. It's the resemblance to your father, of course. I saw a picture of him in a magazine not long ago, and you do look very much like him."

In spite of Reland's friendly intent, Lisa was silent. Norman *had* see her before, and somehow she had wanted him to remember the occasion and not pin everything on her resemblance to her father.

Reland watched her, suddenly anxious. "You don't mind our interest in your father, do you?"

"Of course not," Lisa said. "I'm very proud of my father."

"You have reason to be." Reland smiled and moved away, walking down the path.

Lisa looked after her for a moment. She felt oddly puzzled by Reland. The girl looked so young, so – almost helpless. Yet there was at times a flash of maturity that set her apart from the younger girls. Why didn't she want to go home, when she so obviously loved the very sound of the word?

Well – that was the interesting part of

meeting new people. Everyone had a story, everyone carried both happiness and grief somewhere inside him. And you couldn't find the answers to all the puzzles there were. She'd like to know Reland better. But in spite of the girl's gentle friendliness, there was always – not a wall, exactly; something softer than that. A curtain perhaps. A curtain that Reland hung between herself and the world.

That afternoon and the next morning were busy and Lisa had no time to think of Reland. Just before lunch the following day she went upstairs to take out a tour. The lobby was busy with visitors. When Lisa led her group to the model of the UN and asked for questions, she sensed that someone at the rear was watching her with special interest. People shifted about and a man came toward her whom she recognized as an English teacher she had back in high school. As they moved from one station to the next, she enjoyed renewing an old acquaintance and inquiring about other classmates with whom she had kept in touch. She stepped onto the escalator first, and saw to it that the teacher came onto the steps behind her, so she could talk to him all the way upstairs.

At the council room level, she stepped off and led the tour into the corridor, still talking to the teacher. Not until she was well into the hall did she realize that the sounds behind her were wrong. By now she knew instinctively how the clicking of heels on the hard floor should echo, and the sound today was remarkably thin. She turned quickly, to find that only five people had followed her off the escalator. The rest of the tour had vanished.

After her first moment of dismay she spoke to them quietly. "Our group seems to have become separated. Will you wait here, please, until I find the others."

What on earth could have happened? she wondered, hurrying back to the escalator. How could some fifteen people vanish so completely? And would she know them again if she saw them?

There was no one lingering in the escalator enclosure and she stepped anxiously onto the upmoving stairs. Not until she reached the cafeteria floor did a little girl see her and shout, "Mommy, here she is!" A woman in a red hat came rushing out of the cafeteria to greet Lisa like a lost friend.

"I guess some people who weren't with the tour got on the stairs," the woman said, "and we just followed them all the way up. The rest of us are around here somewhere."

Lisa gathered her flock about her in relief. When they were ready to leave, she glanced in the direction of the cafeteria, hoping no one was watching her dilemma. She was not reassured to find two men standing near the door regarding her with interest – Jimmy Webb and Norman Bond.

"Hello," Jimmy said and came toward her before she could escape. "My favorite guide! Is this a new part of the tour today?"

She made no attempt to answer him, but hurried away to lead her lost sheep down the escalator, her cheeks pink from the encounter. She couldn't help but remember that she had sent Norman a message about no more boners. Those two were certainly a jinx.

Reunited with the others, Lisa took care not to become preoccupied in conversation again, and there were no more misadventures. Her high-school teacher looked as amused as he used to when some bright member of his class had painted himself into a verbal corner.

By the time the tour was over and she got back to the lounge, Lisa could once more tell the joke on herself. The other girls had some stories of their own to tell.

Lizette was excited because a V.I.P. had turned up unescorted on her tour – a well-known senator from Washington. Usually such people were taken around officially by a senior guide. But this man had stepped up to the desk and bought a ticket like anyone else. If someone hadn't recognized him, no one would have been the wiser.

On the other hand, Jeanie Soong had a bored movie star in her group – very beautiful and rude. Everyone had recognized her, but unlike some theatrical celebrities, she was far from gracious. She was with two handsome men and the three had whispered all through Jeanie's talks in the council rooms.

Asha, coming in just then, heard Jeanie's account. "There is a way to end such things," she said. "I stop my talk and stand, saying nothing. I look at the person who will not be still. Soon everyone else looks also and he is ashamed into keeping quiet. Or sometimes I say, 'I am sorry, I did not hear your question,' and the disturber does not know how to answer."

Lisa could imagine how easily Asha, with her cool dignity, could subdue and abash the unruly. So far, she was glad no such trouble had arisen in her own groups.

One of the Dutch girls said, "It's the people who go to sleep that I mind. I try to pretend they aren't there, but it's disconcerting when it happens."

So the day went – off on tour, back in the lounge to remove one's shoes and talk, write letters, or read; then out again. Now that classes were over, Lisa worked Saturday and Sunday too, having her days off earlier in the week. This, she had learned, was a matter of priority. When she had been here long enough and other new girls had come up behind her, she would be entitled to have the week ends off. But right now Saturday and Sunday could be busy days for the Tour Service.

The order in which the girls left at night usually depended on the order in which they came in that morning. There was no set closing time for tours. If it was a busy day, a guide might keep right on after five o'clock.

Lisa found herself working late that same afternoon. When she checked with dispatch after her last tour, the girl at the desk said, "There's a pest around here asking for your release. He says to look for him near the foot of the stairs."

Puzzled, Lisa hung up and went to the locker room to get out of her uniform. "Pest" sounded very much like Jimmy Webb. But when she reached the stairs in the public lobby, she saw that both Jimmy and Norman were waiting for her. Jimmy seemed cheerfully sure of his welcome, while Norman held back a little, taking less for granted.

"I've come to walk you home," Jimmy said. "I don't know who this character is that's

106

shadowing me. We'll ignore him. There's no use objecting because I can blackmail you now. I can tell the other girls about your losing half your tour in the cafeteria."

There was no malice in his words, for all his teasing, and Lisa smiled. "Sorry – but I've already told them. It was too good a joke to keep – after it was over. So blackmail is out."

"That's what I warned Jimmy," Norman said. "I've come along to throw him into the Children's Fountain if that's what you'd like."

Lisa laughed out loud. "All right," she said. "You can both walk me home. I'm sorry I haven't some packages for you to carry."

They went upstairs to the delegates' entrance and out past the big circular pool of the Children's Fountain without throwing anyone in.

8. *Spaghetti for Four*

As the three reached the apartment building, they met Margie hurrying along with her arms full of grocery bags. She wore her short blue coat and was hatless, her blond pony tail swinging as she walked. Interest sparkled in her eyes when she saw Lisa's companions, and without waiting for an introduction she took Jimmy's measure and handed him an armload.

"You look as if you were coming our way," she said. "I hope you don't mind being useful."

Jimmy grinned from behind the tall paper bag she thrust into his arms. "This is what my fatal charm always lets me in for. Little girls make the mistake of thinking I'm the domestic type and a beast of burden, when I'm only hungry."

Lisa made the introductions, and found that somehow they were all going upstairs together in the elevator.

"How did Jimmy know I lived around here?" she asked Norman.

"He probably cornered every guide he met and asked until he found one that knew," Norman said. "Jimmy's tactics are simple, but not subtle. I'll get us both off your hands as soon as he can put that bag down."

It did not work out like that, however. Margie and Jimmy took to each other with apparent enjoyment. Jimmy didn't seem to mind when Margie bossed him around a bit, and she was plainly enjoying herself. By the time they reached the apartment Margie had invited both boys to stay for dinner.

108

"Spaghetti," she said. "And it will be good because I cooked the sauce for hours last evening."

Norman threw a helpless look at Lisa and tried to protest, but Lisa shook her head. "What Margie decides to do, Margie does. And I suspect your friend Jimmy is not going to stand up to her. So please stay. We'd like to have you."

Jimmy, having disparaged himself as the domestic type, was promptly tied into an apron with organdy ruffles. Margie flung off her coat, looking gay in a red pleated skirt and white blouse. In Margie Jimmy had found someone he could top by half a head and he was enjoying the novelty.

"Why I run around with you six-foot Janes, I'll never know," he said, shaking a rueful head at Lisa who was five-four. It developed that Jimmy had grown up with four older sisters and was accustomed to being bossed around the house by women.

Since Lisa and Norman had been banished from the kitchen as being in the way, Lisa glanced at her watch and turned on the radio. It was so late there was barely time to catch her father's broadcast. As Reid Somers's voice came into the room, Norman, who had been glancing at some books on a table, turned around.

"Your father? I've been wanting to tell you how much I admire him. He's my favorite commentator."

"I think he's pretty good myself," Lisa said.

They listened together to the broadcast. Once or twice Norman glanced at Lisa and his new interest was plainly evident. The experience was a familiar one to Lisa. Reid Somers's fans were legion and the family did not always enjoy them as much as he did. Norman was behaving just like another fan.

When a card table was set up in the living room and they all sat down to "slurping" spaghetti, as Margie put it, Norman began to ask questions about Lisa's father and their life in Washington, until she felt more and more like a machine that could only answer questions about Reid Somers.

Yes, she said, her father had known the present Secretary-General years ago in Europe and still saw him occasionally. Yes, it was true that he was writing a book about the United Nations. In fact, the book was getting along toward completion.

It was a relief when a scrabbly sort of tap sounded on the door and Margie said, "That's Bunny Starling's secret knock," and went to let the little girl in.

"Goodness, *we* ate a long time ago," Bunny

said, hesitating hopefully in the doorway, her very freckles standing out with eagerness on her stubby nose.

"That's fine," said Margie. "Then you'll have room for a second dessert. Come in and meet Jimmy Webb and Norman Bond."

Bunny said, "How do you do," politely, her big brown eyes deceptively demure. Lisa noted that Whirly was perched on her shoulder looking brightly around the room. When Bunny approached the table Norman held out a finger, and the little parakeet fluttered off Bunny's shoulder to the proffered perch.

"Look out," Lisa warned. "Whirly bites."

As if trying to live up to his reputation, Whirly pecked at Norman's finger; but it was plain that his heart wasn't in it.

"He likes you!" Bunny cried delightedly. "Whirly, say 'how-do-you-do.' "

"Pret-ty-birrd," said Whirly obligingly and left the finger to swoop over Jimmy's head and perch on a picture frame.

"Should be named Squirrely," said Jimmy, recovering from a quick duck.

"My mother was crazy about birds," Norman said. "We had cages of them at home when I was a kid. She was very good and patient about teaching parakeets to talk."

Bunny coaxed the bird back to her shoulder

111

and looked with interest at the ice cream with raspberry sauce that Margie was bringing in from the kitchen.

"Am I glad I came!" she announced. "I couldn't stand it at home any more. The monster is watching television." She noted the startled look in Jimmy's eyes and explained kindly. "My little sister Mimi has an imaginary playmate. Five is much too old for one and she should be getting over it. Personally, I think she's just not adjusted. Anyway she put the monster in front of the television set tonight and I couldn't see a thing."

Jimmy gaped. "Whose imaginary playmate did you say this was?"

Bunny took her plate of ice cream and sat down on a big green leather ottoman. "Tonight the monster has four heads. That's why I couldn't see. It's really very unhealthy of Mimi."

"Come off it," said Margie. "Stop talking like a psychology book. Don't laugh, Jimmy. Her mother doesn't want her to be encouraged. Though I must admit I'd leave too if Mimi's monster grew four heads."

Lisa smiled. "You can see how insidious it is," she said to Norman. "I'm beginning to catch it too. The monster tripped me up with his tail the last time I went to the Starlings'

112

and I nearly fell on my nose."

Jimmy said, "Sister, let me out of here!" and pretended to make for the door, but Norman regarded Bunny with a matter-of-fact interest.

"Do you suppose I could meet him sometime?" he asked.

"I'll go get him right now," said Bunny obligingly, but Margie waved her hastily back to her ice cream. "Some other time. After all, it's Mimi's privilege to show him off. Let's do without him tonight."

When they finished dessert, Norman remarked that he had noticed carrots in the kitchen and asked if Margie still had the tops around? Carrot greens were retrieved from a pan in the sink and Norman held them under the cold water faucet for a second, then shook them free of all but clinging drops.

"What are you going to do – eat them?" Margie asked.

But Bunny cried, "I know! I know! He loves that!"

While the others watched, Norman made a nest of carrot tops on the kitchen table and Bunny put Whirly down beside them. Promptly the little bird ducked his head into the greens and rolled around happily.

Afterwards, when Bunny had gone reluctantly back to the call of homework,

113

Lisa and Norman took their turn in the kitchen, while Margie and Jimmy turned on the radio and tried some new steps in the living room.

"You don't have to help with dishes," Lisa told Norman. "Just sit and talk to me."

Norman seemed willing enough to have it that way – no organdy apron for him – and they talked idly while Lisa washed and dried the dishes. Then she wiped her hands and turned away from the sink.

"I have something you might like to see," she said, "since you're a fan of my father's."

She went into the bedroom and brought back a framed picture of her father and mother. Norman took it with interest. The picture was not a formal studio photograph, but an enlargement from a news shot, one that was Lisa's favorite. It showed her father helping her mother down from the last step as she left a plane. It had been taken in California where she had flown to join him a couple of years ago. She was laughing down at her husband as he greeted her, and one couldn't help but sense the warmth and fondness that existed between them.

Norman looked long at the picture, missing no detail. "Your mother is very pretty, isn't she?"

"Beautiful," Lisa said. "And the most

serene person you could imagine. Which she needs to be in our family."

"I'd like to meet her," Norman said, studying the picture. "Most women don't know much about serenity these days."

"Perhaps you can meet her when she comes to New York to visit me," Lisa told him. "She says she'll come the minute the press of Dad's work lets up."

Norman handed the picture back. "I'd like that. And of course to meet your father too, if it's ever possible. The two of them look happy together. They like each other, don't they?"

"Why, of course," said Lisa. What an odd thing for him to say.

He noted her surprise. "That's not always to be taken for granted in a marriage, you know. Sometimes I think people can love each other without any real liking at all."

That seemed a strange notion and she wasn't sure she knew what he meant. She felt a little uncomfortable, but before she could take the picture back to the bedroom, he spoke again and she knew he was seeing her as a person now, not just as Reid Somers's daughter.

"You're lucky to have parents like that. My own mother died when I was ten. My father married again a few years later –" He broke off as if he had said more than he intended.

She carried the picture into the bedroom and set it on her side of the dressing table. Was that it? Norman probably had a stepmother whom he didn't care for. She felt sorry for him, and a little curious too. He was not at all like Jimmy, with flashing surfaces to be read as you ran. There was something more behind his quiet air than could be quickly understood.

When she returned to the kitchen she found him at the window looking out toward the Secretariat Building.

"It's beautiful, isn't it?" Lisa said softly. "Somehow it makes me feel tingly just to look at it. I suppose because of all it stands for. I feel the same when the flags are out in the morning and I walk past them. They mean so much."

"I hope so," he said gravely.

His tone startled her. "You sound as if you didn't believe it."

"I *want* to believe." He stared out at the scores of panes flashing light. "But everything before has failed. And there are so many people, even in our own country, trying to undermine what the UN stands for. Why do we always have to move so slowly toward what ought to be obvious?"

"It's like looking at a painting," Lisa said. "You can see it quite clearly and you're sure

116

of what you see. But for the fellow across the room the light falls differently and, he can't see it in exactly the same way. I'm discovering among the girls I work with that each nationality has a different viewpoint and sometimes it's hard to know what really is the truth of the picture."

Norman nodded thoughtfully and there was interest in his eyes. "That's good," he said, "that use of a picture."

"My father didn't say it," Lisa told him quickly. "I thought it up myself!"

They laughed together and Jimmy looked in the door.

"Sounds like good fun you two are having. Suppose you bring the laughs along for a game of Scrabble. Margie is putting out the set and she seems pretty determined about it."

"Oh, no!" cried Lisa despairingly. Playing Scrabble with Margie was a long step on the way to a nervous breakdown. Margie couldn't spell at all and she came up with the most fantastic combinations of letters which she fought to defend. The dictionaries all had mistakes in them, according to Margie, and she seemed to take any correction as a personal affront to her intelligence.

Lisa looked helplessly at Norman and he smiled. "I expect it will do us no good to

117

struggle. I don't mind."

So the game was played and Margie was given her head. Jimmy, enjoying himself mightily, said that of course "crunch" was spelled "krunsh." And nobody spelled apple with two "p's" any more.

It was Norman who finally insisted that they were all working people and it was time to go home.

As they went out the door, Jimmy said, "We'll be seeing you girls again!" but Norman only smiled, committing himself to nothing.

When they'd gone, Margie whirled around the room, gay as an elf, her red skirt flaring. "That was fun, Lisa! I'm glad you brought those two home. Let's ask them over again soon."

Lisa, putting up the bridge table, did not answer. After all, this visit had not been of Norman's choosing and he had not said readily that he wanted to come again.

Margie stopped her whirling and regarded Lisa suspiciously for a moment. Then she flopped onto the sofa, her lower lip stuck out like that of a pouting child.

"I know!" she cried. "You think I'm not good enough for your college friends. You're ashamed of me because I can't spell. And that Jimmy Webb was laughing at me all the time. He was, wasn't he?"

118

Margie was actually believing her own words.

"I'm sure both boys liked you," Lisa told her gently. "Why wouldn't they? You're a very likable person when you're not acting like an infant."

"But I know I'm a dumb bunny!" Margie wailed. "I hated school. And I know I can't spell. So how can I ever date the sort of boys I'd really like to date?"

Lisa sat down beside Margie and put an arm around her.

"I don't think spelling is exactly everything," she said. "You're generous and warmhearted, Margie, and we all love you."

Margie switched her pony tail over one shoulder and chewed mournfully on the end of it. She appeared to be thinking. Lisa left her there and went to get ready for bed. For a while she heard nothing from Margie. Before she got into bed she took some pennies from her purse and dropped them through the slot in the Mexican pig's side. They clinked in with the others that Pedro was saving for her.

"What are you going to buy when he's full?" Margie asked from the doorway, as calmly as though there had been no despair a few moments before.

"I'm not sure yet," Lisa said. "Since he's such a special pig, it will have to be something special." She got into bed and sat up against her pillow. "Margie, I've been wanting to ask you something. Would you mind if I invited a few of the guides over some evening?"

"Of course not," Margie said readily. "If they're college girls I'll just go out to a movie, or something, so you can have the place to yourselves."

Lisa sighed. "Why are you so snobbish about college?"

"Snobbish? Me?" Margie gaped at her. "It's the other way around. The last girl who shared this apartment had all kinds of degrees and things. All she did was try to make me over. She used to apologize to her friends for me. I took it until the time she came home and started to talk about ignorant people in movie theaters who eat popcorn. So I went out every night for a week and brought home a bag of popcorn to eat in bed. I nearly died."

Poor Margie, Lisa thought. She was beginning to understand that chip on her shoulder. But it was hard to keep a straight face. "That seems a little extreme. What happened?"

"She left," Margie said. "And just in time too. Before I died of popcorn. That's why I wanted to get it all over in the beginning when you came. Bob Starling never told me that you were college too. Bunny let it out. But you're really not so bad, Lisa."

"Thank you, Margie," Lisa said. "And let's not either of us be snobs."

Margie had taken the clasp from about her hair and was leaning forward to brush it vigorously as she did every night before she went to bed. Now she straightened and threw the fluffy mass back over her shoulders.

"I never thought about that snob business working both ways, but I guess it does. If your guides won't snoot me, I'd like to meet them. Tell me about them."

Lisa clasped her hands about her knees and began to decide out loud which girls she'd like to invite.

"There's a girl from France whom I like a lot – Lizette Laverne. And there's Jeanie Soong, who is a darling. And –"

"Soong?" Margie was puzzled. "Sounds like a laundryman's daughter."

"All Chinese aren't in the laundry business, any more than all Americans are rich. And there's Asha Dyal, a perfectly stunning Indian girl. I'm not sure she would come, but I'd like to ask her."

"You mean an Indian with feathers?" Margie was really startled now.

"No – with a sari. She's a Hindu girl from India. And of course Judith Johnson, who's one of my favorites. She's not what you'd call college yet, though she's taking night classes and hopes to get a degree later on. She's a colored girl."

"Well, sure," Margie said. "Bring 'em over. I've known Negro kids in school, of course. But I've never met any Chinese or Indians from India. It sounds like fun."

So this hurdle was behind her, Lisa thought, sliding down under the covers. Margie was a darling, really. And her gay informality should help a lot when the girls came over.

After Margie was in bed and had switched off the light, Lisa closed her eyes and listened for a while to the steady hum of the electric clock. When things were quiet that clock practically roared. They ought to invest in a new one. At length her thoughts turned to Norman and his visit here tonight. She remembered the way he'd looked at the picture of her parents.

"They like each other," he had said so strangely.

Yet how true his words were. As she thought more about them they seemed less strange. What Reid and Katherine Somers had *was* special. It was what she wanted for herself some day. And she wasn't at all sure she would ever find it.

9. *Blue Cornflowers*

It was just a week later that she was called to the phone one afternoon in the guides' lounge. "Man's voice," Lizette whispered, her hand over the mouthpiece.

Lisa took the phone. She recognized Norman's voice before he gave his name and she liked the way it sounded over the wire – a good voice for radio.

Would she care to go to dinner and a movie some night next week? he wanted to know. There was a Japanese restaurant he was fond of, and there was a revival of an old Garbo picture playing not far away.

The invitation came as a surprise. Across the room Reland sat at the dressing-table shelf writing a letter. The soft curve of her cheek was visible, and in the glass Lisa could see the faint sadness of her expression. For just a moment she hesitated. What were the ethics in such a matter? But surely the choice was Norman's, and since she would enjoy going out with him, she accepted happily.

She went to her next tour with an unexpected lift to her step. It was fun to have a date to look forward to. She'd really been neglecting the social side – which wasn't a good idea, as Margie kept pointing out. Margie had begun urging her to invite her friends to the apartment.

At home that evening she looked through her neglected dress-up clothes and decided on a gray-blue frock, with tiny blue buds appliqued here and there on the skirt. It had a scoop neck and she could wear the handsome silver and turquoise Indian necklace her father had brought her after a trip to Colorado.

On the night of her date Margie looked her over with critical appraisal. Margie was so odd a mixture of the spoiled baby and the instinctive mother, that her changes never ceased to take Lisa by surprise.

"Wrong shade of lipstick," said Margie. "It didn't matter before – with you taking all those sheep out on tour. But when you're going somewhere with a man –" she shook her head. "Too much blue for your complexion. Wait – I've got a true red here I haven't even opened. It's a sample a cosmetics' salesman gave me. Try it."

Dutifully Lisa removed her old lipstick and tried Margie's bright, true red. She was smiling a little as she looked at herself in the mirror, thinking of Margie's disrespectful labeling of the people who took tours. So far she had not been able to get Margie anywhere near the UN. In Margie's mind the whole thing had something to do with using one's brains and this was an occupation Margie claimed she abhored. Let other people mess up the world – that job wasn't for her.

Lisa was not sure the new lipstick made as earthshaking a change as Margie declared, but it was possible that it did look a little better.

"At least you've got sense enough to use a light flower scent," Margie approved. "You're not at all the *femme fatale* type."

"Well, thanks a lot," said Lisa doubtfully.

"I'm not insulting you. If I know men – that Norman Bond likes wholesome girls."

Lisa was even less inclined to like the word "wholesome." So often the wholesome thing was also pretty dull. But there was Norman at the door and she had to go.

At least he seemed to approve what he saw. He helped her with her light fall coat and Margie wished them a nice evening enthusiastically as they left.

On the way to the restaurant in a cab, Norman told her he'd had a good friend in college who was Japanese and he learned to like the food at that time. The cab dropped them uptown and they climbed a flight of steps into an old brownstone house. There an amiable Japanese gentleman greeted them and showed them to a table. The ceiling of the big dining room was high and there were interesting Japanese prints around the wall. The tables were filled with other diners plying chopsticks.

Lisa and Norman had a pleasant corner table where they could see the rest of the room. Lisa had never eaten a Japanese meal and she was delighted with the clear soup, the tiny salad that looked like flower petals on the flowered plate, and the delicious shrimp fried in egg batter. There was a plump earthenware pot of green tea from which Lisa filled tiny handleless cups again and again.

While they were eating the shrimp, a Japanese waiter came to light the burner on their table and set fat to melting in a frying pan. Then he brought a huge blue and white platter of beef and vegetables for *sukiyaki* and let Lisa admire the ornamental pattern of the arrangement before he turned meat and vegetables into the sizzling pan and stirred skillfully with chopsticks.

Norman could eat with chopsticks, but they were beyond Lisa, though she made a brave attempt to conquer them.

"How do you like the girls you're working with in the guide service?" Norman asked, when she'd given up chopsticks to use a fork with the salad.

126

"Very much," Lisa said. "Of course I'm just beginning to know some of them. They are all interesting and they seem to have stories behind them. I want to invite a few over to the apartment soon."

"Jimmy called Margie up the other day and she mentioned this gathering. What girls do you plan to invite?"

"I'd like to have Jeanie, the Chinese girl. And Lizette. And Judith Johnson, though she's not one of the new girls. I'd like to invite Asha Dyal, the Hindu girl, too, but she's a bit hard to approach. I've even wondered if she might be a little of what Margie calls snooty."

"Probably not when you get past her reserve," Norman said. "We Americans have a knack for easy friendliness with strangers that not all other peoples have. Or even want, for that matter. And we're too apt to term snooty anyone who doesn't leap into our laps like a happy puppy dog."

"Anyway, I'll invite her," Lisa said. She sniffed the delicious odor of the *sukiyaki* hungrily. But there was no hurrying – they had to wait while the food cooked.

"How do you like Reland Munro?" Norman asked casually.

"I don't know her well," Lisa admitted. "The girls are all fond of her and she seems very likable. But she strikes me as not being

127

altogether happy here."

"She still gets homesick," Norman said.

"But she doesn't want to go home. She told me so the other day."

"I know. My mother came from Edinburgh and I think she too never got over being homesick for Scotland. When I was on leave from Germany I flew to Scotland and visited my grandparents for the first time."

"How nice," Lisa said. "Did you meet Reland while you were there?"

"No – not until later when she came to New York. My grandparents knew her parents and when she decided to come to the States my grandmother wrote and asked me to look out for her. She gave me a little of her story."

Lisa waited, not wanting to ask more than he cared to tell. She had gathered from the other guides that Reland, for all her appearance of quiet friendliness, had not talked about herself very much or attached herself to any one girl as a special friend.

"She's had a pretty bad time," Norman went on. "She was engaged to a boy she went to school with and everything was set for their marriage. Then he was killed in a highway accident that was someone else's fault."

Lisa shivered. "No wonder she looks so unhappy at times."

"My grandmother wrote me that all she could think of was to get away, where she wouldn't have to meet sympathetic friends, wouldn't have to be in the places where they'd been happy together. So she came to New York. She's not over it yet by a long shot. That isn't something you can run away from. I suppose she talks to me a little because I already know and because there's the bond of Scotland between us."

Lisa thought of Reland in pity. How terrible to lose the person you loved when you were so young that all your life together still lay in the future.

"Of course I'm telling you this in confidence," Norman said after a moment. "I'm not just gossiping. That time I listened to you when Jimmy and I crashed your tour, you struck me as the sort of girl Reland ought to have for a friend. When you spoke of inviting some of the girls over, I wondered –" he broke off, hesitating.

But the *sukiyaki* was ready and the waiter returned to ladle rice onto their plates and cover it with the savory mixture of beef and vegetables. Lisa nibbled a tender wedge of bamboo, but her thoughts were on what Norman had been telling her.

"Of course I'll be happy to invite her over with the others," she said when the

129

waiter went away. "But do you think she'll come?"

"I'll persuade her to," Norman said. "This is awfully good of you, Lisa. Though I knew you'd do it."

Suddenly she didn't want to talk about Reland. Norman had known about her plans ahead of time through Jimmy, and she didn't want to think that perhaps this date had been planned to give Norman a chance to broach this subject to her, get her cooperation.

"Tell me about your radio work," she said, changing the subject. "Are you in it for good?"

"I'd like to be. The important thing for me right now is to make myself a place in this UN work. And save some money too. When I went into the army I could be really independent of my family for the first time and I liked it. What I'm working toward is enough experience to be able to do interviews for the UN abroad. There are lots of on-the-spot recordings made, you know."

"Sounds exciting," Lisa said. "And I can understand what you mean about independence. I wanted to get away from home too."

He looked surprised. "With parents like yours?"

"I'm terribly fond of my parents," she

130

said quickly. "It's just that everything has to revolve around Dad. And that's as it should be. But I have a feeling that I don't want to be lost in his shadow. My brother Ted will do all right because his interest is in science. He doesn't even know there is a shadow. But I haven't any special talent. I don't know just who or what I am. If I stay home and Dad gets me a job, I'll be – engulfed."

Norman looked kind and understanding. She could see why Reland might easily turn to him with confidences she would not give anyone else.

"You'll find out who you are," he said. "Give yourself time."

She asked about his friend Jimmy then and mentioned how much Margie had enjoyed their coming over.

"Jimmy liked Margie too," Norman said. "They seem to share the same sort of lightheartedness. Sometimes I envy Jimmy's talent for having a wonderful time under any circumstances and never letting the unpleasant touch him. He can be as carefree about atom bombs as he is about the choice of a tie. And I suspect Margie can equal him there."

They went on to talk about the UN after that and Lisa found that Norman's feelings

131

about its work matched her own. He was more impatient and inclined to be angry with those who impeded progress. But he kindled just as she did and it was good to discuss these matters on common ground.

She tried to give him some of the points her father had often made at home – that any change which had to do with ideas took a long while, if people were not to be forcibly indoctrinated – and that wasn't the UN way.

But Norman wasn't satisfied to move so slowly. "There's so little time," he said, as he had once before. "We can't afford to be as slow as we've been in the past. The tide is rising too swiftly. And part of the current is against democracy."

That was sobering and Lisa knew from listening to her father that it was true. But the United Nations was one of the chief forces democracy had on its side.

They finished dinner with rice cakes and more green tea. When they went outdoors the fall evening was still light and the brisk air felt wonderful.

"This is the best time of all in New York," Norman said. "Maybe there are no autumn leaves underfoot, no wood-smoke smells, the way we have in Connecticut, but the city takes on a sparkle. There's nothing like Fifth Avenue on a fall evening."

"It's a shame to go inside and sit in a theater," Lisa said, breathing the tangy air.

"We needn't, you know," Norman seemed pleased. "I was hoping you might like a walk better. We can do the movie another time when it rains."

Lisa couldn't help a sense of pleasure because he sounded as though they might do this again. Tonight was even nicer than she had expected.

He matched his steps to hers as they turned down Fifth Avenue. All along the way lighted shop windows were jewel cases of luxury. This was one of the great avenues of the world, selling goods of all the world. This was something free enterprise and democracy could achieve for a country.

The noonday crowds were gone and though there were still cars swishing by and other strollers out on such a night, it was a pleasure to walk the pavements with no hurrying crowds to shoulder through. Now and then they stopped to look at some fantastically beautiful display and Lisa would sigh wistfully and wish that Pedro were crammed with twenty-dollar bills. Norman played the game as she would not have expected him to.

He said, "No – not the hat with all that cabbage on it. And not the slinky one of black jet. But the one at the back with the blue cornflowers on the brim – that's for you. Matches your eyes."

She laughed ruefully. "Cornflowers! I know – Margie told me before I came out tonight that I was no *femme fatale.*"

"She's right," he said. "I've never yet met a *femme fatale* that I wouldn't run from screaming. They scare me even when they look at me in the ads. I like undramatic women with nice dispositions."

As she had with Margie, Lisa felt a bit of feminine pique. How dull it sounded to be an "undramatic woman with a nice disposition." She wasn't sure she'd want to live up to such a description.

As they crossed side streets they could glimpse brilliant neon lights clustered toward the west and Broadway. But Fifth Avenue had been kept clear of such clutter and retained its dignity. Lisa liked the avenue at night and she sensed that Norman did too. Indeed, as they neared Rockefeller Center she had the increasing conviction that they felt alike about many things. The memory of Reland, the faint twinge of guilt, receded. This feeling that was in the air tonight had only to do with Norman and herself.

At Rockefeller Center they walked down the wide esplanade between high buildings, where people strolled beside the long stretch of flower beds. They found an empty bench and sat down.

"We can watch the world go by here," Norman said. "It's a little like the lobby of the General Assembly Building."

They sat with the great shaft of the central building rising above them, almost as high as the Empire State. Lisa, watching the crowds go up and down the walk, became aware that Norman was looking, not at the passers-by, but at her. She glanced at him almost shyly, wondering what he was thinking.

"It's not just the resemblance to your father," he said. "I still have the feeling that I've seen you somewhere before."

She smiled at him, pleased that he was remembering. "You told me the green plant was in memory of someone who died in a war."

For just a moment he was puzzled. Then his eyes lighted. "Of course! The girl in the Meditation Room that day. I remember thinking that you looked like someone it would be nice to know. What unexpected tricks life plays!"

They sat for a little while in silence and Lisa felt oddly close to him – as if she had known him for a long time and they understood each other completely.

It was Norman who stirred on the bench

beside her and began to speak in a matter-of-fact tone. The moment slipped away and Lisa knew that for some reason he had turned from it. Yet the moment, the feeling had *been*. And perhaps it would come again in the future.

"What are you going to do after your year or two as a guide, Lisa?" Norman asked.

That question was always coming up. "That's one of the things I hope this job will help me settle. Most of the girls find interesting positions after this one. Some of them even go to work in the Secretariat."

"What about radio?" he asked.

She shook her head emphatically. "That's the last thing I'd try! I've heard radio-radio all my life. I want to get away from it. With my father so big in the field, I could never be really on my own in radio."

"Why not?" he said. "Don't forget I've heard you on a tour. Your voice is better than most women's for recording and you're good at talking to people. You have an enthusiasm that's contagious and it gets into your voice."

"That awful first day!" She shuddered. "No, radio's not for me. People would say that my father pulled strings. And that's not what I want. Whatever I do, I want to do it myself."

They sat for a little while in silence before they returned to the avenue and continued toward Forty-second Street. But Norman did not leave the subject at once.

"Maybe Reland is right about American women," he mused. "She says you're all too busy being career girls to have time for your main job."

Lisa blinked. "You mean the wife-and-mother line? But we manage that too."

"Do you? Not that Reland was criticizing – she's never unkind. But she says Scottish women know more about making a home than American women seem to."

"You should see my mother," said Lisa. "All her married life she's lived for Dad. Everything is for his success, his comfort. And she's an American woman."

"Isn't that the way it should be?"

She knew he was teasing her now, but she answered seriously. "I don't think so. Asha was talking about *purdah* the other day. You know – the state some Indian women still live in, behind veils and closed doors, never speaking to any man not related to them, living only for their husband and children. In a way my mother lives in a sort of *purdah*."

Norman put his head back and laughed out loud. "I'll bet she'd be surprised to hear you say that. And do you think she's been unhappy?"

"Of course not. But she is *her* sort of woman. I'm *my* sort. That European-Asian wife may be wonderful for her husband, but isn't she frustrated when it comes to developing herself in her own right?"

"Hear, hear!" Norman said, drawing her to a stop on the curb as the light turned red. "But why all this driving ambition? What is it that you want from life, Lisa, that you're so afraid of frustrating?"

She couldn't answer that. She didn't really know. She felt ruffled, and her pleasure in the seeming closeness between them had evaporated. It seemed only an illusion now.

Forty-second Street lacked the sparkle of Fifth Avenue. The neon signs looked gaudy and the small shop windows were crowded with too many articles. Lisa was beginning to tire. She must have sighed without realizing it, because Norman glanced at her contritely.

"How inconsiderate I've been. Here you spend your days walking and I take you on a busman's holiday. Lisa, I'm sorry."

There was no way to explain that it was not only her feet but her spirits that had lagged. They were nearly back to the apartment, so she told him she'd loved the walk – which was true enough, and invited him in, since it was not very late.

But now he seemed restless again, almost as

138

if he were eager to get away. He said good night quickly at the revolving door. In the elevator she let weariness and an odd feeling of depression engulf her. It was disappointing to find someone you warmed to, and with whom you seemed to have a lot in common, only to discover that somewhere along the way your roads turned unexpectedly and went in opposite directions. The moment of closeness she had experienced in the esplanade had been only of her own imagining. Norman had not really shared it.

10. Control Room

Lisa saw nothing of Norman in the next few days. She was busier at work than she had been since she started. The G.A. – the General Assembly – was in session and visitors thronged to the UN by the thousand. By nine in the morning when the doors opened, club groups began arriving, wearing cards pinned to their lapels. Of course many of these had come to attend meetings and would soon disappear into the depths of council chambers, or the visitors' galleries of the Assembly auditorium. But other groups, and hundreds of individuals, came to spend the entire day at the UN and found time to fit in a tour.

The guides had changed to their dark blue uniforms and now Lisa had her own uniform which she wore with a feeling of pride. It was fun to stand out as one of the UN guides, whose fame was spreading far beyond the walls of these buildings. The bulletin board in the guides' lounge carried clippings of write-ups they'd had in several other countries.

Of course, as Mrs. Warren reminded them from time to time, they mustn't let the uniform go to their heads. Their job was important, yet it was still infinitesimal in the vast scheme of the UN. The girls had to hold a neat balance between a sense of their own worth, and a sense of humility about what they were doing.

By now Lisa's plan to have a few of the girls over some evening had crystalized. Lisa gave Margie a little of the background of each girl so she would be interested in them as individuals and be less likely to balk at any strangeness.

Of those Lisa told her about, Margie seemed antagonistic only to Reland. While Lisa had not mentioned the things Norman had confided to any of the other guides, there had been no reason to hold them back from Margie. She had not expected Margie to take the attitude that because Lisa had gone out once with Norman, Reland was somehow a menace. Margie trusted to instinct and emotion, and set very little store by mere reason and good sense.

"I could tell that you two were just right for each other," she announced, to Lisa's wry amusement. "This Reland had better keep hands off, I'd say, or she's liable to get her heart broken all over again."

"Don't be foolish!" Lisa cried, laughing. "In the first place Norman and I barely know each other. And in the second, Reland is still in love with that boy who died. She talks about him quite often to Norman."

Margie remained unconvinced. "Never trust a girl with a broken heart. She's always looking for a rebound so she can patch it together again."

Lisa let the subject drop and avoided it thereafter. She and Norman had not managed as well as Margie thought. Besides, how Norman and Reland felt about each other was their own business. She repeated this to herself several times firmly.

One morning a few days before the Friday when the guides were coming over, Lisa ran into Jimmy Webb in the corridor. He seemed

141

happy to see her.

"Just had a blinding inspiration," he said. "How would you like to watch the recording of a show in the radio department? Not that this sort of thing is new to you, but –"

"I'd love it," Lisa said readily. Unbidden the thought of seeing Norman came into her mind.

Jimmy turned from his course to walk beside her. "How about this evening then? We'll be working after you finish and it should be interesting. Just come in and ask for me."

There was no reason to hesitate, so she said, "Thanks, Jimmy. I will. See you later," and went on to the dispatch desk.

One of the girls put down the phone and looked at her appraisingly. "Feeling strong today?"

"I'm not committing myself," Lisa said lightly. "There's a trap."

The girl nodded. "Have a look behind you. High-school crowd. Think you can manage?"

Lisa did not trouble to turn. She had taken young people's groups out before and she always enjoyed it. Often they were more interested than older people and they asked sharper questions. Besides, there was always a teacher along to help maintain discipline, if that was necessary.

"No problem," Lisa said. "Of course I'll take them."

But when she started across the lobby toward the glass doors, she understood why the girl at the desk had been doubtful. These were older boys and girls and the boys looked somewhat on the rough and noisy side. Lisa glanced about for the teacher in charge and for a moment thought that the group was alone. Then a girl who looked not much older than those in her class came toward her, a strained, anxious expression on her pretty young face.

"Are you the guide who will be taking my group?" she asked. And when Lisa nodded, she hurried on. "I'm a substitute, but this trip was planned a long time ago and I agreed to bring them over. They're terribly undisciplined though."

The girl looked upset almost to the point of tears and Lisa's only thought was to reassure her. "Don't worry. High-school groups like these tours. We won't have any trouble."

But as the group of twenty jumped up to crowd somewhat rowdily through the doors, she wondered if her optimism were misplaced. Obviously there were three or four clowning boys who were the leaders, with a few of the girls egging them on. When Lisa was introduced, one of the boys whistled, but she ignored him and smiled as she would at the members of any tour when she led them off in the direction of the plaster model.

There only a few seemed interested in what she was saying. The rest talked and laughed among themselves and the little teacher was helpless to quiet them. Lisa went through her explanations at the model and asked for questions. Silence fell and they all stared at her expectantly – as if she might ask herself a question and prove entertaining.

Then one boy said, "Hey, what you doing tonight, beautiful?"

Again she ignored the outburst of laughter and led them on their way, walking briskly ahead, aware that the boy who had spoken was trying to catch up with her. Again there was a whistle or two and she heard the young teacher twittering nervously in a futile attempt to get the group in hand. Obviously this couldn't go on. This smart aleck had to be dealt with, or the tour would end in complete confusion.

As she waited for them to gather near the Peace Bell, she glanced briefly at the boy who had placed himself near her. He was painfully homely, with too many freckles and big ears. Being a clown was probably his only way of getting the attention he wanted.

They did not quiet down to listen to her

this time, but kept on talking and she had to raise her voice to be heard.

"This young man," she said, "has asked me what I was doing tonight." They heard her then. The silence was sudden. "I'm not doing anything tonight," she went on, looking at her tormentor.

He rose to the bait, fairly wiggling his enormous ears. "How's about a date then, girlie? How's about a date?"

Bluff, she thought, remembering Reland's advice. Don't let them know you're mad and shaking a little too. The silence was complete, and she spoke into it gently.

"Thank you so much," she said. "But the boys I go out with have to be at least ten years old. And they have to be able to act their age."

She was glad they were in the neck of the building where the yelps of laughter wouldn't go echoing up the elevator shafts clear to the Secretary-General's office. The boys whooped and the girls squealed – all except a few who looked uncomfortable and ashamed of their companions. The boy who had spoken to her blushed all over his large face and his very ears seemed to droop. She could feel almost sorry for him. But he had it coming. She spoke again firmly and the uproar quieted down at once, everyone ready for more fun.

"All right," she said, "the game is over. And before we go one step farther we'd better understand each other. If you want me to I can give you a good tour. These buildings are worth seeing. What is being done here affects your lives and mine. I happen to believe that the job I'm doing is important and I won't waste it on anybody who isn't interested. It's up to you. If you like, we can go ahead and I'll do my best to make this interesting. If not, then we'll disband the tour right now. May I have hands? How many would like to take this tour?"

Several hands went up at once. The rest of the group shuffled, looked at one another sheepishly, and then one by one every hand went up – even that of Big Ears.

There was no trouble after that. She had won their respect and they were ready to follow wherever she led. After that she threw herself into the job of interesting them and did her level best. What was more, they listened now with intelligence and real interest. When she called for questions in the Security Council room, Big Ears himself came up with a very good question. She answered pleasantly and after that he dogged her footsteps loyally and once when a couple of girls took to whispering in the back row, he scowled at them fiercely.

146

The thanks they gave her when the tour ended in the basement lobby were warm and sincere. By that time they all seemed to like her and she found herself ready to like even the roughest one of them. But when she'd returned to the lounge, she went to the alcove behind the curtains and stretched out on a cot.

She felt drained and limp. An experience like that could certainly take it out of you emotionally. In spite of her success she felt more depressed than elated. She wanted to talk to no one for a little while, but just to let her energy seep back before she took out the next group.

From beyond the curtains that cut off the rest of the lounge she heard the other girls talking. Not much of the low buzz of conversation reached her until Reland's voice broke clearly through, a note of pleasure in it.

"Has anyone seen that Garbo picture that's being revived? Norman has asked me to see it with him tomorrow night."

One girl started to talk about the picture, but Lisa ceased to listen.

She closed her eyes and told herself she didn't care. This was nothing new. Norman had taken Reland out a good many times in the last six months. She was tired and depressed, or she wouldn't give it a thought. But all through her arguments a traitorous voice kept whispering: "Remember how perfect it was that night on Fifth Avenue? He said cornflowers would look just right on you. For a little while you had a feeling that you belonged together and liked each other. And you thought this might come again. You thought the Garbo picture was for *you*."

Now she wished she hadn't promised Jimmy to visit the radio department tonight and watch a recording being made. She might run into Norman there, and she didn't want to see him right away.

"Oh, act your age!" she told herself crossly. "You're as bad as that boy on the tour."

It was a difficult day because she had to make more of an effort than usual. When she was through she phoned the apartment and told Margie she'd be late to dinner and not wait. Then she followed the concourse corridor that led to the big space sectioned off for radio and television.

A T-shaped hallway accommodated offices, recording library, master control room, and a line of recording studios. A young man in shirtsleeves and sweater went by and she asked him where she would find Jimmy Webb. He gestured and said, "Studio Six."

As she approached the door she heard the

squealings of a recording tape being run backwards. Jimmy was in the small control room alone and he looked up and beckoned her in.

"Hi," he said. "Take the chair over there in the corner. Then you can watch and nobody will fall over you."

Lisa sat down in the corner chair and looked around. The little control room had green walls and ceiling made of sound-proofing material. Two opposite sides were formed by big plate glass windows. These overlooked broadcasting studios. You could look through the windows from studio to studio, right down the line.

Radio studios were far from unfamiliar to Lisa. She'd been sitting in on broadcasts since she was a little girl. But most of her father's programs were live, and this was something a little different.

Jimmy grinned at her as he worked at the recording machine opposite one glass window. "Having a little trouble here," he said. "What do you think of this introduction?"

He switched on the machine and as the tape turned she heard Norman's voice coming from a big gray loudspeaker at her elbow.

"In French . . ." said Norman, and a voice spoke words in French. "In Spanish . . ." Again there was an interlude of the language.

"In Russian ... in Chinese ... and in English –" There was a roll of drums and the name of the program from the United Nations was given. Then an interview began and Lisa heard Norman talking to a farming expert who was discussing problems of crop-raising in Israel.

A man and a woman came into the control room deep in discussion and stopped to listen. After a few moments the man waggled a finger at Jimmy to stop the whirling tape.

"You'd better take that 'yeah' out," he said.

Lisa recognized his voice and knew he was Dave Morgan, who covered most of the important UN broadcasts that went out "live" to listeners. Apparently he was in the production end too, and the girl with him was an assistant in that department.

"There are five of those 'yeahs,' " Jimmy said. "I counted. Norm must have been carried away."

"Leave in a couple for the sake of being natural," Dave told him, "but let's get rid of the other three."

Jimmy's fingers moved like lightning. He ran the tape one way, then the other, while it squealed and yelped, located the exact space of the "yeah" and cut it out, splicing the tape together neatly. In one place the farm expert coughed and that came out too. When Jimmy was through, the interview ran along more smoothly, with no evidence of tampering. This was certainly a different process from live programs, where whatever happened, happened. Lisa had not realized such trouble could be taken over a final effect.

In between his activities, Jimmy introduced Lisa to Dave Morgan and to Molly Haines, and Molly took time to tell her what a good job she thought the guides were doing. Then they went back to discussing Norman's introduction, while Lisa looked about again. There were loops of discarded recording tape on the floor, and even bits and pieces of it stuck to the wall by means of Scotch tape. Probably these were sections still to be spliced in.

While the others were talking, Norman came into the studio and Lisa wanted to shrink into her corner, pretend she wasn't there. She didn't want him to think she might be here in order to see him. He noted her over Dave's shoulder and looked faintly surprised. But he nodded in a friendly way as he listened to what Dave was saying.

"We'd like that drum roll to come in under Norm's voice," Dave was explaining to Jimmy. "Then, Norm, if you'll give it a bit more build-up to a climax, it should be right."

"Want me to try it again?" Norman asked.

Dave nodded. "Just the introduction."

Norman left the control room and Lisa, watching through the plate glass window, saw him take his place at a table with a microphone on it. Jimmy rolled his chair across a few feet of space between recording machine and the control console which sat on a long wooden table before the window. He took a test of Norman's voice, while the red needle on the panel swung back and forth.

"Stand by for recording," said Dave into the mike that connected with the studio. Jimmy spun his chair back and forth between dials on either side of the room. Dave said, "Ready – recording – cue!" and pointed at Norman, who went into his introduction.

The red needle danced to the vibration of his voice, while Jimmy reached for this dial and that. But there still wasn't enough build-up to please Dave, and Norman ran through the introduction a couple of times more before it was right. When he finished he came in to hear the play-back. Afterwards he said, "See you later," to Jimmy, waved a casual hand at Lisa, and went off.

After that, to her own annoyance, she found

152

it hard to concentrate on the interviewer and his guest who took their places in the studio for a recording. This day had been a distracting one and her attention kept wandering. Nevertheless, it had been nice of Jimmy to invite her here and she thanked him when the recording had been made and she could leave.

As she rose he said, "Hey, wait a minute," and leaned over to pick up a curl of brown recording tape from the floor. He made a dramatic business of tying it about her wrist in a bow, and pulled her suit sleeve over it. "Souvenir," he explained as she laughed and went toward the door. "That's one of Norman's 'yeahs.' "

She got away as quickly as she could and went home. Margie had kept dinner warm for her in the oven and she ate hurriedly at the kitchen table. Something pricked her wrist and she saw she was still wearing the strip of tape. She pulled it off and tossed it into a wastebasket. She was hardly interested in keeping one of Norman's "yeahs" for a souvenir.

Tomorrow she would come straight home and catch up on chores. She'd wash her hair and set it. She'd rinse out stockings, mend rips, sew on buttons. Tomorrow she would make herself so busy she wouldn't know what happened to the time. Tomorrow night Norman was taking Reland Munro to a show.

11. *West Meets East*

On the following evening, however, Lisa's plans were somewhat delayed. Margie was out of sorts. All through dinner and afterwards, she complained about women with neglected skins who came to cosmetic departments and wailed because the creams and lotions they bought didn't make them look like some young movie star overnight. She was, she announced, altogether tired of crotchety customers and being asked forty times a day where the ladies' room was.

Lisa wiped dishes and listened with one ear. It was hard to attend to Margie and keep herself from thinking about Norman and Reland. Would they walk down Fifth Avenue tonight, or sit on a bench in Rockefeller Center?

"I don't see why," said Margie, banging pans in the sink, "you can't invite Jimmy and Norman over again. Jimmy called me up once, but he just talked awhile and I didn't get a chance to ask him."

"Norman is out with Reland tonight," Lisa said.

Margie regarded her accusingly. "There – you see! The rebound."

Before Lisa could answer, she heard Bunny's scrabbly knock on the door.

"I'm not sure I feel up to the Starlings tonight," she said. "I'll see if I can get rid of her quickly."

She opened the door a crack and looked into the hall. Not one, but all three Starlings stood there. Mimi was crying with big deep sobs, Bunny's lower lip stuck out, and even Carol wore a gloomy expression. Here, apparently, was a major disaster and there could be no closing the door in their faces.

"What's happened?" Lisa cried. "Have you had an accident? Are your parents home?"

"Blow your nose, Mimi," Bunny said, and marched ahead of the others into the apartment. For once she had left her bird at home, and Lisa noted with relief that Carol closed the door right after Mimi, so there was no length of monster to be let in.

"Tell me what's happened," Lisa demanded again.

"I want Margie!" Mimi wailed.

Bunny nodded soberly. "We especially want to tell Margie."

Lisa waved them toward the kitchen and looked at Carol for an explanation.

"It *is* a disappointment," Carol admitted, following the others, "but it's not as bad as Bunny is making out. Bunny enjoys emotional scenes. And of course Mimi doesn't really understand what it's all about. She's acting up because Bunny got her started."

It was apparently hopeless to try for a plain statement, so Lisa herded the three into the kitchen, where Bunny promptly plastered herself against the window that looked out toward the Secretariat building.

"We could have gone there Saturday!" she said tragically. "It was all planned. Daddy was going to take us. And I was going to get a set of United Nations flags to take to school. But now we can't go because he's got an old customer and has to be tied up on Saturday."

So at least no one had been maimed, Lisa thought in relief. It was just a childish disappointment which Bunny was building into oversize proportions.

Margie turned away from the sink, regarding the girls with some suspicion. "So?" she said.

"Margie will take us," Mimi piped, widening big brown eyes in a way that made Lisa suspect that she had been coached by Bunny and was speaking on cue.

"Does your mother know you're here?" Margie asked, unmoved by Mimi's wide-eyed look.

Bunny and Mimi began to talk very loudly at the same time and Carol made an effort to make herself heard above them. The result was bedlam.

"Qui-et!" cried Margie. "Let Carol talk, for goodness' sake."

Silence fell abruptly, but it was Bunny who talked. "We came out very quietly so as not to disturb Mom, on account of she is writing a speech she has to give to her club on Saturday. That's why she can't take us. It's a very important speech about child psychology from a parent's point of view, and she says not to furnish her with any new material right now."

"She wouldn't like us to be doing this, of course," Carol said. "I just came along to restrain Bunny."

At once bedlam burst out again and Lisa shook her head and put her hands over her ears. You wouldn't think three little girls could make so much noise. This time Margie simply turned her back and began wiping out the sink. When she ignored them silence gradually fell and Bunny nudged Mimi.

"You'll take us, Margie, won't you, huh?" Mimi said as if a button had been pushed.

"You said this Saturday was your day off," Bunny pointed out.

"It is my day off this week, and I will certainly not take anybody anywhere," said Margie, without turning around. "I'm going shopping. Besides, I've never been to the UN and I'm not going to spoil my record now. I refuse to be improved."

"Aw, Margie, we wouldn't improve you," Bunny wailed. "You'd just take us – that's all."

"A lot of fun that would be. Why can't Carol take you?"

"Because," said Carol readily, "my two younger sisters are too unruly. And Mother says she can't have Bunny disrupting the workings of the entire United Nations." She looked at Lisa wistfully. "We were going over especially to take your tour. It's really too bad. I was looking forward to it."

"Well, I won't do it," Margie said and hung up the dishcloth with an air of finality.

The three girls seemed to wilt like thirsty flowers. Mimi gave a last deep sniffle and Carol slipped a tender arm about her.

"Don't you cry, Mimi. There'll be another time."

"Of course there will," Margie said briskly. "You can just as well go the following Saturday."

"But that's years!" Bunny wailed. However, she made a brave effort to straighten her shoulders. "Well, come along, kids. I really didn't think Margie would do us like this. I didn't think she'd be so crool."

They started toward the door, but Mimi turned back for a last try. "I wouldn't take the monster, Margie. I'd leave him home."

"Well, I should think so!" Margie exploded.

"You can see she's in a bad mood," Bunny whispered audibly to Carol, and they all looked at Margie warily as they tiptoed into the living room, as if in the presence of someone who might bite.

Lisa chuckled softly, watching them go. "A really fine performance. It's a shame to see it come to nothing. And it wouldn't kill you, Margie. You might even enjoy it. Why don't you break down and take them?"

"So you're against me too," Margie said. "Oh, all right – I suppose I'll have to. Hey, kids! Maybe we could go over after lunch and then take a tour in the afternoon. That way I can shop first thing in the morning."

They swooped back upon her with cries of joy. Bunny and Mimi hugged her and Carol looked on with quiet pleasure. Plans were made at the top of everybody's lungs and Lisa went off to wash stockings. She'd done her good deed for the day anyway.

She felt tired clear through tonight and had no desire to sit up and read as she often did before she fell asleep. After Margie had gone to bed and the lights were out, Lisa snuggled down beneath a blanket and listened to the muffled roar of New York that could always be heard through the open window. Now and then she could distinguish the tootling of taxicab horns, or the sound of a boat on the river. Sometimes a plane roared high above the canyons of Manhattan. But mostly the sound was a muted murmur, like the voice of a giant who muttered and never slept. And of course there was always that silly alarm clock.

She burrowed deeper and pulled the covers to her ears. But other aspects of New York came through in memory. In another apartment a radio was playing the instrumental of an old song. The words whispered in her thoughts. *These foolish things . . . remind me of you.*

She got out of bed and closed the window gently, so Margie wouldn't waken. Then she got back in and tried to give herself a lecture.

She was not here to get involved. Not with anyone. She was here to find out about Lisa Somers. But a perverse voice kept asking whether this was an uncomfortable part of finding out about Lisa. Were these things, too, something she had to discover about herself, even though she resisted such self-discovery?

Fortunately, daytime thoughts were often brighter than those of the night and by morning something of her melancholy had vanished.

When Friday came, she felt more cheerful and was looking forward to an evening with the girls at the apartment. Lizette was the only one unable to come. Jeanie, Judith, Asha, and Reland had all accepted. There had been a brief hesitation on Asha's part, but she seemed genuinely pleased to be included. Reland had looked for a moment as though she might draw back into the shell of shyness that sometimes enveloped her. Then she seemed to reconsider.

"Thank you for asking me, Lisa. Norman said you might and he thinks I ought to go out more."

Margie had cheered up too, in spite of her date to visit the UN the next day, and had gone to work making numbers of decorative little sandwiches.

Jeanie and Judith were the first to arrive and Margie was entranced with Jeanie's appearance in her silk gown of pale sea green. The third girl to arrive was Reland.

She brought a gift for Lisa and Margie. There was no hint of sadness about her tonight and she looked touchingly eager to enjoy the evening.

"My mother makes these for a hobby," she told Lisa, handing her the package. "I don't suppose you drink tea the way we do at home, where there's always a pot to be kept hot. But I hope you can find a use for it."

Margie watched with the interest of a child while Lisa unwrapped the package. Her eyes were round with bewilderment when the large, blue quilted object was revealed. Lisa set it on a table, where it stood up of its own bulk.

"It's awfully pretty," Margie said. "But what's it for?"

Mother had one at home, so Lisa knew. "It's a tea cosy. And a really beautiful one."

"Well, I do like my tea cosy," Margie murmured, "but what do you do with it?"

Jeanie Soong chuckled. "I've seen them in English homes. You put it over the teapot to keep it warm."

Lisa saw Margie's blank look and hurried with her thanks. The moment she finished, Margie burst in.

"It's a honey! And I know just the place for it."

She bore it away and Lisa, hearing Bunny's special knock on the door, went to answer it. Bunny had not been invited, but you could leave it to the middle Starling to know when something interesting was in the wind.

Lisa opened the door and found Asha standing there, with Bunny beside her, looking completely smitten.

"I meet this young lady downstairs," Asha said in amusement, "and she is kind enough to bring me here. She tells me you are good friends with her."

Tonight Asha wore a smoky-blue sari, shot through with silver threads, and Bunny hardly took her eyes away as she spoke to Lisa.

"Please may I come in? Oh, *please!*"

Lisa could hardly refuse so heartfelt a plea. "Of course," she told the little girl. "But you'll have to be quiet, Bunny, and not talk all the time."

Bunny nodded vigorously, her lips sealed. Indeed, her breath was so taken between Asha, and Jeanie in her Chinese dress, that she could not talk at all. She plumped herself on an ottoman between the two and stared at them in open delight. It took her several minutes to recover. Then she broke right into Lisa's introduction of Asha and Margie.

"Are you a princess?" she asked Asha.

The Hindu girl smiled. "No, I am only a

schoolteacher."

"Oh, you are not!" Bunny cried. "I know lots of schoolteachers. You're just fooling me."

"It is true that I am not yet a teacher," Asha said, "but I hope to become one when I go home to India."

"What a fine thing," Jeanie said. "Where are you going to teach? In Delhi, where you live?"

"No – I wish to go to the villages. So many, many teachers we need in the villages of India. That is where most of our people live. Yet only a few can read and write. This is the reason I have come to study in the United States. I wish to get the feeling of your democracy to help me in my teaching."

"Are you getting what you came for?" Judith asked.

Asha made a graceful gesture with her hands. "It is not so easy. But I try very hard to understand American ways. It seems to me sometimes that Americans are not so willing to understand India." She broke off apologetically. "You do not mind that I say this?"

"Of course not," Lisa assured her. "I've been wanting to ask you questions for a long time. What do you mean exactly?"

"It is difficult to explain," Asha said. "I

know how it is true my people have much to learn from America. We lack ability to get things done with the quickness of the American people. We are behind in matters of machinery, literacy, science. We are beginners to run our country as a united whole. But because we are behind in some ways does not mean that we are unintelligent. Sometimes foreigners come to India and treat us impatiently as if we are stupid children just because we do not at once accept everything they tell us."

Jeanie leaned forward, slim hands clasped about her knees. "In my country it was this way also."

Asha nodded and went on. "We feel there can be more willingness to understand our culture. We do not like it that America sometimes behaves as though we have need of her, but she has no need of us. Perhaps there are certain things the West can learn from India."

"The peoples of the East know what India means to the world," Jeanie said gravely.

"Such as what?" Margie was blunt.

Asha smiled courteously. "Here I am your guest. I do not come to criticize."

"We can't do rope tricks, or charm snakes like the Indians can," Bunny pointed out, and everyone laughed.

"Do go on," Lisa said before Bunny could request a demonstration of snake charming. "This is something we need to hear." She glanced at Reland, who was listening with interest. Judith looked eager to speak, but she too waited.

Asha smoothed a fold of her sari over her shoulder. "Perhaps you do not know that many of my people have a feeling of abhorrence for what they regard as Western immorality."

"Hey, wait a minute!" Margie cried, squirming to the edge of her chair. "If you mean Americans –"

"Ssh!" Bunny hissed. "Give the princess a chance!"

"Thank you," Asha said and went quietly on. "I will explain. In our religion many Hindus believe that it is wrong to kill any living thing. So it is shocking to us that you of the Western world destroy life in the eating of fish, fowl, beast. We believe that all man-made death is evil. Only God has the right to take life. To us the atom bomb is a sin against God. That is why Gandhi's philosophy of nonviolence has received support in my country."

"I'll go along with you on that," Judith said. "But it seems to us that if you'd kill some of the cattle that roam all over India, you'd

166

have food to help the starvation problem."

Asha lifted her hands despairingly. "You cannot say this to a people who believe so differently. No more than I can say to you that if you Americans will stop this senseless hurry-hurry-hurry, then you will not die so much of heart failure. Why must you hurry? Always for the material thing – the thing you can see and touch and buy in a store."

"But you have to admit," Reland put in gently, "that such practices are good for a country. In Great Britain too, we sometimes cling too long to the old ways."

"But when in this hurried life," Asha asked, "do you take time to think, to pray? It is surely not moral to omit the spiritual side from life."

Bunny caught the word "pray" and burst in. "Our family goes to church every single Sunday!"

"And between those Sundays, do you take time for meditation, for prayer?"

Bunny looked uncertain and again Reland came to the defense of the country she was visiting. "Many Americans do. I don't think it's fair to say there is no spiritual life in America just because it is different from India."

Asha smiled calmly, but she went on, caught up in her own feeling for what she was saying. For the first time Lisa could see the fire that might flash in this girl who always seemed so cool and self-controlled.

"My people," said Asha, "know that time stretches back for eons, and ahead for untold ages. To us, what is happening now is important only if we do our best for our future life. When we look at it in this way, a ten-o'clock appointment tomorrow morning does not always seem important. Is this not so?"

"Just the same," said Judith, "if that ten-o'clock appointment isn't kept, then perhaps your students don't learn to read, and things that are wrong continue in India for still more eons."

"The lack of compromise is one of the things that has held India back," Asha agreed.

"But you said we were immoral," Margie persisted. "Gosh, I ate a ham sandwich for lunch. Am I supposed to call that immoral?"

"I will grant that it is your custom to eat flesh," Asha said. "But can you understand that for others it might seem very wrong?"

"What about prejudice in India?" Judith asked. "I mean your discrimination against groups of your own people because of religion or caste divisions. You criticize America for intolerance, but aren't you guilty too?"

"I am sorry to say much prejudice still exists," Asha admitted, "in spite of our changed laws. When an entire people has been taught something for centuries, so that it is ingrained as a matter of religion, of emotion, it is very difficult to change quickly. For example, the Hindu Brahman is taught from babyhood that he is of a superior caste. I am taught this as a child. I pray many times for humility, yet there are moments when I feel foolishly superior because I am born of a fortunate group. It is hard to uproot this thing which exists inside me. How much harder then to uproot it when there is no desire to do so. As a teacher, I wish to help create this desire for change. This is something I am trying to learn from America. You do indeed have prejudice among your own people. The world watches you critically for that. Yet there is a surprise for me when I come here."

"A surprise?" Lisa asked.

"In India I am told it is very much worse than what I see here. I have even heard that the colored peoples are still bought and sold, that there is no justice for the Negro in any court, that all white Americans hate the colored man. Since India is a nation of colored peoples, this is a bad thing for us to hear."

"My gosh!" Margie cried. "If that isn't the silliest thing I ever heard in all my born days! Why look how happy we are to have you and Judith here tonight."

Lisa suppressed a smile, wanting to hug Margie.

Asha nodded. "This is a good thing to see. I can take home to my people the truth of what I find here in New York. That many races live here in friendliness and on an equal basis. I can tell them there is now on the wind in America a wish to change which is heartening to see. It is something my country must learn."

Jeanie Soong spoke as though she were puzzling out loud. "Sometimes it seems that all countries are top-heavy in some way. Perhaps India leans too far when it comes to mysticism, and America depends too much on industrialism. An exchange of our specialities might be a good thing."

"Like I can cook," Margie said. "And Lisa can –" she hesitated and Lisa laughed out loud.

"Come on, Margie – tell us what it is I can do."

"Well, you're very intelligent," said Margie kindly.

There was laughter and then a little silence, broken by Bunny.

"How do you stick on that thing in the middle of your forehead, Asha?"

The serious mood was over and Asha and Bunny were deep in a discussion of pigments and caste marks – worn now mainly for decoration, Asha said – when the doorbell rang.

Bunny took it upon herself to answer before anyone else could stir and came back in a moment with a wide grin on her face.

"Hey, Lisa!" she announced. "Your mom's here!"

12. Bunny Meditates

Lisa ran to the door to greet her mother with a hug. "Mother, what a wonderful surprise! And you couldn't have come at a more perfect time. Girls, I want you to meet my mother."

Mrs. Somers, trim in a gray suit, her gray hair topped by a little black hat, came smiling into the room, quietly at ease as she always was.

Lisa introduced each girl in turn, feeling proud of her mother's appearance and poise. Mrs. Somers explained that she had suddenly found a gap of time when her husband would

171

be out of town briefly and she could get away. So she had packed an overnight case and caught the first train to New York. There'd been no time for letters or phoning – here she was. And she could stay till Sunday. She hoped she wasn't intruding on their party.

Margie offered at once to give up her bed and sleep on the day bed in the living room. But Mrs. Somers had already checked into a hotel and had no intention of disrupting their living arrangements.

Then, with her sure instinct for reaching out to the quietest person in a room, she found her way to a chair beside Reland Munro. Reland responded readily to her friendly interest.

"Your mother's a doll," Margie whispered as she and Lisa went out to the kitchen to get refreshments. "No wonder you got yourself brought up right."

This, Lisa realized, was a high compliment and her sense of happiness over the evening increased. Things were going very well indeed. It was wonderful that Asha had let down her reserve and talked more freely than she ever had at the UN. And Reland seemed to be enjoying the evening too. For Norman's sake as well as Reland's, Lisa was grateful for that.

Like everyone else, Bunny warmed to

Lisa's mother. She pulled her ottoman over to sit near her, munching contentedly through a half dozen small sandwiches. Before Beth came to summon her home, Bunny had invited Mrs. Somers to join their group tomorrow when Lisa took the girls on tour. Lisa half expected Margie to back out when this new arrangement had been made, and leave the escorting job to her mother. But apparently the evening had made Margie curious about the UN, and she stayed with the original plan to take the Starlings over herself.

When the guests had gone, Margie offered to pick up and put things to rights, while Lisa sat down for a visit with her mother. But Mrs. Somers insisted on helping too, so they all chatted together as they went back and forth between living room and kitchen.

"Where did you put the tea cosy?" Lisa asked Margie as they passed each other at the kitchen door. "I want to show my mother the gift Reland Munro brought us."

"It's in the bedroom," Margie said. "I put it over the electric clock."

"Over the clock!" Lisa went into the bedroom and sure enough, there on the little bed table stood Reland's impressive tea cosy, completely hiding the electric clock. The clock's crackly hum was almost indistinguishable, well muted by the quilted covering.

Mrs. Somers laughed in delight. "A wonderful idea! I should have one just for that purpose myself."

"It makes it a little difficult to read the time," Lisa said, picking the cosy up to show her mother what a really handsome piece of work it was. "Reland is Scotch-Irish – from Edinburgh. Her mother makes these. It was sweet of Reland to bring it to us."

Mrs. Somers turned it about in her hands, admiring the workmanship. "I like your little Reland. She's a sweet child and a bit lonely in the rush of New York, I think. Though I gather she is very much in love with an American boy who works in the radio division over at the UN."

Lisa put the tea cosy back over the clock. "Oh? Did she tell you that?"

"Not in so many words. But while we were talking she told me about him and kept quoting things that he'd said. Her feeling was quite evident. Do you know the young man?"

"Yes," Lisa said, "I know him." She was aware that Margie had come to the door in time to hear her mother's words. She hoped that Margie would say nothing, but that wasn't Margie's way.

"There!" cried Margie indignantly. "What

did I tell you? It's that rebound thing. Reland's just got to have someone to love. So of course it would be Norman. I hope he's got sense enough to see it coming and get out of the way."

"I think he's quite fond of her," Lisa said quietly.

Her mother looked puzzled and Lisa didn't want to explain. She began to ask questions about Dad and Ted, and about how Dad's book was coming. Mrs. Somers was kept busy with home talk until late.

Lisa went downstairs and saw her into a taxi. For a few moments she stood on the sidewalk, watching until the car turned west. It was lovely to have her mother here for even so short a visit. She hadn't fully realized how much she missed home until this moment. When she went back upstairs it was with a contented feeling about the entire evening. It had gone better than she could have hoped.

Only one thing bothered her – the remark her mother had so unwittingly made about Reland. But did that really matter? None of that was her affair.

The following day her mother came to the UN for lunch and they had a good visit, with so much to talk about that they kept jumping from subject to subject, never quite finishing a topic, but enjoying it all enormously.

After lunch Mrs. Somers returned to the main lobby to wait for Margie and the Starlings, while Lisa went back to work. When dispatch called to say that her party was waiting, she hurried eagerly upstairs.

Bunny's wave was enthusiastic, but by now Margie looked doubtful and awed, rather than excited, by the surroundings.

"Don't expect to sell me a thing," she muttered to Lisa, as the tour assembled at the glass doors.

The Starlings had eyes for no one but Lisa. When she moved they ran at her heels, and when she stopped they gathered under her nose, not at all reluctant to let the entire tour know of their personal acquaintance with a UN guide.

At the model Lisa ran a quick eye over the group. Here she had learned to make a mental count which might help later, in case she lost any of the tour. She noted that there were other children along today, three boys and one little girl about nine who was already eyeing Bunny speculatively. Mrs. Somers stayed well in the background and Lisa knew that her mother was trying considerately not to catch her eye and make her self-conscious.

At Lisa's, "Please follow me," they all moved into the corridor, with the children doing a Pied Piper at her heels.

The Starlings had checked their coats downstairs and were dressed up in their Sunday best, with crinoline petticoats holding out their bright skirts. Mimi was having a little trouble with her skirt. Every now and then she would raise the whole thing practically to her eyebrows and then pat it out into place to make sure it stood out properly. Carol gave her several reproving looks, but Mimi was more aware of her skirts than she was of the Peace Bell when Lisa stopped to talk about it. Once Lisa thought Bunny was behaving rather oddly, but she had no time to figure out why. It was Margie's job to keep an eye on the girls. Besides, Mother was there to help, if necessary.

Margie, looking not much older than Carol, wore a blue dress that set off her fairness. Her pony tail had an extra jounce to it today, in spite of her expression of determined boredom. Lisa, trying to break through and catch her attention, saw that she listened to the story of how the delegates from more than sixty nations had given silver coins which Japan had formed into this bell as a gift to the UN.

Not until Trusteeship did Bunny's problem become evident. At first all went well in the council room.

"The statue of the young girl you see on the wall to your left was carved out of a single block of wood," Lisa told them. "Her body was made from the trunk of the tree and her upstretched arms are the branches. She represents mankind reaching toward hope in the form of the bluebird above her head."

There was a little squeal from Mimi, quickly hushed by Carol, and Lisa saw the whole tour look past her toward the windows. Without turning she knew what was happening. Transparent curtains hung across the great windows beyond the horseshoe table, and you could see the river through them. A ship was passing and Lisa knew it made a beautiful picture, gliding silently, slowly by, quite close to the window. But while everyone else's attention was on the ship, Lisa caught the sound of a clear, unhuman little voice saying, "How-do-you-do." Oh, no! Not Bunny's bird here at the United Nations! Bunny ducked her head and whispered to something out of sight and Lisa tried frantically to catch Margie's attention. But Margie was looking bored again and had closed her eyes after the brief distraction of the ship. Mother was at the other end of the row, where she could not help.

The rest of Lisa's talk in Trusteeship was somewhat wooden. Her mind was filled with the sound of wings she didn't want to hear. The thought of how hopeless a task it would be to recapture a parakeet in one of these big rooms was dismaying.

When the group had filed back to the corridor, she hurried after Bunny.

"Give it to me," she said in a low voice.

Bunny looked at her in round-eyed innocence, hand in pocket. "Give you what, Lisa?"

"That bird!" Lisa insisted. "Give it to me right away, or I'll have to ask the guard to take you back to the entrance and put you outside. What do you think the Secretary-General would say if he knew you'd brought a parakeet here?"

Evoking such awesome authority did the trick. Bunny took her hand out of her pocket, bird and all, and handed Whirly over. Lisa closed her fingers gently but firmly about the silky little body.

There was no chance to hide this interlude from the rest of the group. Some of the other children had seen the bird and crowded about Lisa with cries of delight. But now that she had the tiny creature in her hand and could feel its heart thumping under her fingers, she was at a loss as to what to do next.

It was Mrs. Somers who solved the problem. She unlatched the top of her wicker handbag and held it out as calmly as if she were accustomed to using it as a bird cage. Lisa put the parakeet in, and the lid was securely latched. Everyone laughed in relief.

The tour went on.

When they entered ECOSOC Lisa went ahead to choose a section of seats for her group. Margie sat beside her charges in the front row, yawning openly, and Lisa felt sure that she heard little of the beginning of the talk on the Economic and Social Council. This, however, was the part the children loved best and Lisa gave it everything she could. One example she used was a story which always seemed to appeal to the younger members of a tour.

"In long-ago times," she told them, "when map makers came to what they regarded as the limits of the earth – knowing nothing of what lay beyond in unexplored areas – they would draw fantastic creatures over the unknown waters and territories and put in the label: 'Here Be Dragons.' "

"There aren't any dragons!" denied a small boy who had been hanging on her words.

Lisa smiled at him. "Oh, yes, there are. That's what I'm coming to. If we drew a map to show the living standards of the world's inhabitants, we would have to mark a great many places with dragons of misery.

Poverty and hunger and disease are some of the real life dragons the United Nations is fighting. And children are helping a great deal in this fight.

"By now UNICEF is a word that means the same in any language. One little boy who saw it so many times in connection with the milk he was given, thought it was the word for cow. As you probably know, these letters used to stand for the United Nations International Children's Emergency Fund. Now it's a permanent thing and we call it simply the United Nations Children's Fund. But we keep the letters UNICEF because they are known everywhere. Because of this fund, children all over the world are being given a better chance for health and happiness."

She was speaking directly to the children now, the Starling girls and the others who were there with their parents.

"How many of you boys and girls know," she asked, "about what American children have been doing all over the country on Halloween to help the Children's Fund?"

Only one boy said, "I know. Last year I collected fifty-eight cents all by myself."

Lisa nodded, smiling, and went on to tell how the idea had started several years ago in one small American town. The children had gone out in Trick or Treat costumes and had collected eighteen dollars for the Fund. In a more recent year $275,000 had been collected by the children of the United States and sent through UNICEF to work for the children of the world.

"Here's something for you to think about," Lisa said. "The cost of a comic book will give a child in Korea several glasses of milk. The cost of an ice-cream cone will help protect an Egyptian child from tuberculosis. And the price of a candy bar can save a child in Chile from diphtheria. Right now, all over the world, there are thousands of children who might have died of disease or starvation, but who are alive and strong because of the Children's fund. This is one of the big things the United Nations is doing."

She paused, aware that the adults too were listening attentively. She was startled to see tears in the eyes of one woman, and when she glanced at Margie, she found that her boredom had vanished. Margie was blinking, and blowing her nose. But it was Bunny's look that really arrested Lisa's attention. It was as though a light had come into Bunny's plain little face, brightening every freckle from some inner source. The little girl sat there raptly, not moving when the others got up to leave.

Lisa touched her shoulder. "Come along, Bunny. We're moving on now."

But Bunny's attention was on faraway matters.

"What is it?" Lisa asked gently.

This time the little girl started and seemed to return to her surroundings. "I was doing like Asha said. I was meditating."

"That's fine," said Lisa, "but I'm afraid this isn't exactly the place for it."

Bunny's new excitement spilled over. "We can do it too, can't we, Lisa? I mean there are lots of children in our building and we could get together and go out and collect for the Children's Fund on Halloween."

Margie had turned back in time to hear. "That's a wonderful idea, Bunny! Of course you can, and I'll help too."

From Margie this was surprising.

"We'll have a meeting," Bunny said. "We'll have a meeting and organize."

Lisa shooed the two after the rest of the tour, and several times after that she had to call Bunny back to the present.

When the group disbanded in the basement lobby, everyone was especially warm about thanking Lisa and expressing their interest in all she had told them. Mrs. Somers stood back until the others had gone and then came over to add her own words of praise.

"I'm proud of you, dear. That was very well done. I wish your father could have heard you."

Mrs. Somers restored Whirly to his owner and the little bird seemed none the worse after his trip through the UN in a wicker handbag.

Lisa stayed a moment longer to reprove Bunny for bringing the bird with her.

"Why *do* you do such things?" she asked, sounding a little like Beth.

Bunny stroked Whirly's head with one finger. Her answer was matter-of-fact.

"I expect it's like Mom says – I like being dramatic. You know – I'm the in-between one, with a beautiful younger sister and a clever older one. I have to do *something*."

"I'd suggest," said Lisa, "that you pick something more sensible next time. After all, while getting Whirly lost in the General Assembly, or somewhere else, might be dramatic, it wouldn't be very constructive."

With this Bunny agreed cheerfully. After all, she'd had her moment in the spotlight. And now she had something really important to think about.

13. Broadcast

Sunday evening, after Mrs. Somers had taken her train for home, Bunny came in to consult Lisa about a plan for organizing the children of the building for Halloween.

She wasn't letting any grass grow between her toes, she announced. "But Mom says for me not to go getting the kids together till I know what to tell 'em. What do I do first, Lisa?"

"I think," Lisa said, "that the first step is for you to come over after school one day this week and I'll see if I can get permission to take you on a V.I.P. tour."

"What's that?" Bunny demanded.

"Perhaps I could take you upstairs personally, as we sometimes do with Very Important People and —"

"I know!" Bunny cried. "Let's go see the Secretary-General!"

"That's not exactly what I meant," Lisa said, smiling.

But now Bunny was off down a side road. "Have you ever seen him, Lisa? I don't mean just around the building. I mean right up in his office at the top of the Secretariat."

Lisa shook her head. "I haven't even seen his office. I wish I had, but the guides don't have much chance to get up there."

Bunny seemed plainly disillusioned, but she recovered and listened as Lisa explained.

"What I had in mind was to take you to see someone in the U.S. Committee for UNICEF. They're the ones who are in charge of this Halloween idea. You could find out all about it right at headquarters. I think that's the best way to work, since October is getting along and you'll have to do some planning before Halloween."

Bunny assured Lisa that she'd be over on Monday the minute school was out. She was as good as her word and Lisa was ready for her when she arrived.

"We have an appointment," Lisa told her as they rode up in the elevator together. "Miss Barnes of the Committee says she'll be very glad to talk to you. Of course all this is usually done by mail. But since you live so close and are a bit late in starting –"

"And since I'm a personal friend of the guide!" Bunny added.

They left the elevator and turned down a long corridor that cut the offices into two sections. The rooms on either side of the hall had a share of those hundreds of glass windows that made up the sides of the

186

Secretariat building.

Miss Barnes was waiting for them. She was young and her eyes danced as she looked at Bunny. You could tell right away that this Halloween project was important and exciting to her. She took a big pumpkin-yellow folder from her desk to place before Bunny. A jack-o'-lantern grinned from the cover and the UNICEF seal marked one corner – a child drinking a glass of milk, set against the olive-wreath emblem of the UN. Across the folder the lettering read: TRICK OR TREAT – A NEW AMERICAN HALLOWEEN FOR THE WORLD'S CHILDREN.

Miss Barnes spread the contents of the folder out on her desk and Bunny exclaimed over each new item. There were pumpkin-yellow identification tags to show that the children who rang doorbells were on official UNICEF business. There were yellow bands that could be folded around milk cartons used to hold the money collected. There were also several booklets with photographs showing the work UNICEF was doing. Mimeographed sheets gave suggestions for organizing this special sort of Trick or Treat in any community or neighborhood. Teen-agers as well as children were joining in the project and it seemed that there was much less mischief in the places where this sort of Halloween was being celebrated by the young people.

"Oh, look!" Bunny cried, spreading out a big colored poster.

Miss Barnes nodded. "Some towns have held poster contests ahead of time and that was one of the winners. You can make your own posters if you like and put them up in buildings and stores around your neighborhood."

"Does this mean we won't get candy or anything?" Bunny asked, wistful, but ready for sacrifice.

"Of course you will." Miss Barnes was sympathetic. "Most people think you children who work at this deserve something for yourselves too. So that part of Trick or Treat stays the same. But there's one important matter you'll have to take care of. In New York City children under eighteen have to be accompanied by a grownup."

This didn't stop Bunny. "Margie will help," she told Lisa with assurance.

"In New York," Miss Barnes continued, "you also have to be sponsored by a church, civic, or youth group. Do you think you can manage that?"

Again Bunny was sure. "There's a mothers' club right in our building. I'll sic Mom onto 'em right away. She says the young should be given a part in neighborhood doings – so

188

here's her chance."

Miss Barnes thought there would be no problem at all with Bunny on the job and promised every assistance the committee could offer. By the time they left the office Bunny was bubbling with plans and Lisa felt encouraged by the way wheels were beginning to turn.

After work on Wednesday of the same week, Lisa changed from her uniform and came out to the stairs to find Jimmy Webb and Norman Bond waiting for her. Jimmy greeted her in his usual casual manner. "Surprise! I phoned Margie this afternoon for a date and, this being her day off, she's invited both of us to dinner. So we've come to escort you home."

Lisa rose to this unexpected turn with a smile. Of course they were welcome, she told the two. She was glad they could make it. Inwardly, however, she was dismayed by her sudden sense of pleasure at the sight of Norman. She didn't *want* to feel that way at seeing him. And she suspected Margie of plotting.

Norman seemed aware of her surprise and shook his head ruefully. "I'm afraid our respective roommates are given to impulse first and consideration last. Are you sure this is all right with you, Lisa?"

"Of course she is," Jimmy said. "How

could she help but be delighted to have two such irresistible fellows over for dinner?"

Lisa smiled and let it go at that. Jimmy did most of the talking on the way home, while Norman walked along at Lisa's side seemingly lost in his own thoughts, paying little attention to Jimmy's sprightly chatter. They were following the sidewalk on the United Nations side and once Norman looked up at the Secretariat building.

"I like it at this time of day," he said.

Lisa knew what he meant. The huge glass sheet that was the side of the Secretariat reflected the buildings and sunset sky of the opposite scene in one great panorama. Below, the flags of the nations fluttered in the breeze.

"It always seems to reflect the world," Lisa said softly.

When they reached the apartment building, Stan, the doorman, grinned at her and shook his head. "Those Starling kids are up to something again. You better brace yourself, Miss Somers, – it's happening in your place."

Lisa sighed. "Oh, goodness! I bet I know!"

When they reached their floor and turned down the corridor, they could hear the uproar from the apartment. As Lisa slipped her key into the lock she heard Bunny's shrill voice shouting everyone else down and knew that her guess was right.

"Prepare yourselves," Lisa warned Norman and Jimmy. "I think Bunny is holding a meeting of the building's children in our apartment."

It was difficult to get through the door because it opened upon an overflow of small boys sitting cross-legged in the little hall. They scrambled over one another to get out of the way and the three newcomers stepped across sprawled legs and baseball bats, barely missing a pair of roller skates. There must, Lisa thought, be twenty-five children in the room.

Bunny, apparently the self-appointed chairman, presided from the kitchen stepladder. A wooden chopping bowl was balanced upside down on her knees, and now and then she pounded the bowl with a wooden spoon to obtain order. Behind her Margie lounged in the far hall, looking sweetly young in a gay apron printed with daisies. Margie was obviously having the time of her life. She saw Jimmy and the others and waved, mouthing words they couldn't hear through the uproar.

Bunny saw them too and screamed at the children. "Hey, you guys! Get offa the sofa and let Lisa have it!"

There was a scrambling and further piling up on the floor and Lisa led the way to the comparative oasis of the sofa. She stole a look at her companions and saw that they both appeared slightly stunned.

When everyone was settled the meeting continued. Apparently the mothers' club had been what Bunny called "alerted" and was willing to cooperate. So the adult end was being taken care of. Beth had said the children could go ahead and make plans that could be put before the club.

"We have to take the inishative," Bunny said.

Whatever that was, the children were willing to take it. By now the discussion had reached the matter of costume and Carol was waving her hand to get the floor.

"Maybe," she said, when her sister had waved the spoon at her, "we could all dress up in the costumes of the United Nations. I should think that wouldn't be too hard to –" but she was at once drowned out by screams of approval. This idea went over well, and the children began to buzz among themselves about what they would wear until Bunny pounded spoon against bowl to restore order.

"I now want," Bunny announced at the top of her lungs, "to interduce Miss Lisa Somers, who is going to tell you all about what UNICEF means." She beamed at Lisa, who stared back helplessly.

Jimmy chortled. "Well, come on, Miss Girl Guide. Let's see you do your stuff."

There was no help for it. Lisa wriggled her way up from the sofa and found a spot where she could stand without anyone right under her toes. As she rose, Mimi, who was over near Margie for safety, being smaller than the rest, announced in her piping voice that Lisa was a guide at the UN.

"They know that," Bunny said impatiently, and Mimi added, "She's standing right on my monster's head."

Lisa glanced down automatically and the children whooped with delight. Everyone in the building knew Mimi's monster and played up to it. It was Norman who saved the day just as Mimi opened her mouth for a real protest.

"You don't have to worry," he told the little girl. "You know he's a very strong monster. He won't mind holding her up."

Mimi looked doubtful, and Bunny said hastily, "Go ahead, Lisa. Tell 'em!"

The roomful quieted down to a moderate extent as Lisa began to speak. Four or five small boys continued to punch each other, but all the little girls were raptly attentive. She chose one of the most touching stories that she used when she took children on tour. It was about a little boy in Indonesia who lived far from any city. He had a terrible disease that made big sores all over his body, and it got so that he couldn't even walk and cried all day long. He was growing thinner and his mother knew he would die pretty soon if no help came to save him.

"That little boy didn't realize he had friends like you across the ocean," Lisa said into sudden quiet. "The UNICEF truck came through in time with its doctor and nurse. The wonderful new medicine made that boy and many others like him well. Now he's strong again and can play like other children. He knows that American girls and boys who are helping UNICEF are his friends and he will never forget them."

It was a simple story and she told it simply. But with this group of children as with the adults the other day, she could sense that she had moved them.

"It's a fine thing that you too are going to help on Halloween," she said as she sat down.

Norman leaned toward her under cover of the spontaneous applause. "You do that very well. You've given me the glimmer of an idea." He waggled a finger at Bunny to get the floor.

Bunny waved her spoon at him. "That's Norman Bond, kids. He's a real radio announcer at the UN. Keep still now and listen to him."

Norman made no attempt to stand. He was tall enough so they could all see him, even sitting down.

"There's not much time left before Halloween," he said, "but if you get to work right away, it might be that I could get you a ten-minute spot on a show we'll be broadcasting early next week. Lisa could tell the story she just told you. And one of you boys who is a good talker, and perhaps Bunny, could represent this group and tell about your Halloween plans. If you're interested, I'll see if I can fix it up for you. I might even work out a sort of script to keep you on the track."

Lisa tried to protest his suggestion about her part, but a deafening and unanimous response drowned her out. The excitement mounted and would probably have bulged the walls of the apartment, if the phone had not rung just then with a request from an impatient mother who wanted her offspring home before the soup got cold.

The meeting broke up informally and all the Trick or Treat volunteers except the Starlings streamed out of the apartment, leaving a wake of bubble-gum wrappers, rubber bands, misplaced sweaters, one roller skate and a lost turtle behind them. Margie rescued the turtle and put it in a deep flowerpot for safekeeping, till Bunny could restore it to the owner. Then she rushed out to look in the oven at her dinner.

Mini began to wail that the monster had been absolutely mashed flat and Bunny looked at her in disgust. "If you didn't have any more sense than to bring him in here with all those boys –"

But Norman said gravely that if Mimi would just blow on him he'd pop right back to normal. Monsters always responded to blowing. So Mimi blew and the monster swelled until everyone had to move out to the kitchen to give him room. Bunny had to hold the door open for quite a while before they got all of him back across the hall to the Starlings' apartment.

"He's green tonight," Bunny said. "That means he's happy, so Mimi needn't worry. When he's unhappy he turns pink. He'll be wonderful to take along on Halloween if he likes what we're doing."

"I think I'm turning purple," said Jimmy when the Starlings had gone. "With yellow spots. Count me, somebody."

But even Jimmy had to be serious about what the children were doing. Margie was excited over the Halloween plans and thought Norman's suggestion was wonderful. But with the uproar over, Lisa made her objections to Norman's scheme heard.

"No radio for me," she said. "I'm allergic to it."

Norman looked both surprised and disappointed. "Why do you say that?"

She knew that her reasons for feeling as she did tied into the strong urge she had to be something herself; something that wouldn't be a mere imitation of her father. But there was still more to it than that.

"I'd be scared to death," she said. "I don't want to suffer that much." She remembered only too well the one time when she had faced a microphone in school for a special program that was being broadcast. She had nearly frozen with mike fright. As her father's daughter she had felt doubly disgraced over her faltering effort. Talking from a platform, or to a group of people on a tour was one thing; broadcasting to unseen thousands was something else. The very fact of her father's fame got in the way.

"In that case," Norman said, "we'd better drop the whole thing. I'd want to build this around you as a UN guide. If you won't let me, then that's that."

"It's probably all wasted effort anyway," Jimmy said. "The minute somebody out in the Pacific starts shooting at somebody else, there goes the whole United Nations. Then what good is your Children's Fund or anything else?" He sounded quite cheerful about the whole thing.

Lisa caught him up quickly. "A whole lot of good! There will be thousands of people who grow up believing in a free world and in what the United Nations is trying to do just because of UNESCO and UNICEF and the rest. The director of UNICEF out in the East says Asia is not only sick because it's poor, but poor because it's sick."

Jimmy said, "Look, lady, I live in the middle of it all day. It's not my headache."

"Have some more baked beans," said Margie placatingly.

Lisa took some beans absently and went right on.

"The thing I can't understand," she told Jimmy, "is why you work at the UN if you don't believe in it."

"I didn't say I don't believe in it. It's just that I can't do anything about it and I'm not going to get upset."

It did no good to become indignant with Jimmy, but Lisa was a little angry.

"A fine thing if we all gave up like that! If we all did nothing. But we don't give up. We keep trying and we never take no for an answer."

"Exactly," Norman said. "We don't take no for an answer, and we never stop trying. So you *will* be on the program, Lisa?"

She stared at him helplessly. "Honestly, I'd be no use to you. I'm terribly afraid of a mike. I'd flop so resoundingly –"

"You know," Norman said, "these kids are on the right track. They don't want other kids to be hungry and sick. In some ways it's as simple as that. And if you think about the children the way you were doing just now, you'll get over being scared of microphones. The important thing isn't whether you live up to your dad's name – it's the good you'd be doing."

He had found the one way of reaching her. She felt cornered, trapped. Oddly enough, Norman's words roused in her a desire to try. She hated to be defeated by so foolish a weakness. And yet –

"You'll be all right," Norman assured her, sensing that she wavered. "I'll rehearse you myself. We'll make it all failure-proof."

In the days that followed Norman made good his promise to the children. The ten-minute spot was procured and he worked out a script. What was more, he put Lisa thoroughly through her paces. He wouldn't let her read her part, however.

"Just talk it," he said. "This is something

you do dozens of times a week. Open your mouth and the words will come. Forget about you and your father. Forget that mike. It's what you're saying that matters."

He made her feel that she had to rise to the occasion and prove that she wasn't being petty about this.

Bunny and Dick, the ten-year-old boy chosen to take part, met Lisa in the studio a half hour ahead of time on the afternoon of the broadcast. Norman had been rehearsing them at home and the children were both confident and excited. For their sake Lisa did not dare reveal her own nervousness. But as the second hand of the studio clock ticked toward the moment when warning lights would go on outside the studio door, her mouth felt dry and her palms damp. This ten-minute spot would be live as well as recorded. When their part was finished, the program would be continued by a young woman who was interviewing a guest.

Dave Morgan, running the show from the control room, raised his arm and brought it sharply down, pointing at Norman. They were on the air.

Norman did a smooth job of introducing the program and telling a little about the Halloween project that was becoming so popular around the country. Then he asked

Bunny and Dick about their special plans. Bunny had no inhibitions and her clear voice went out over the airways without hesitation. Dick spoke up too, though not quite so readily, and Norman brought out the account with further questioning.

Lisa listened, sitting on the edge of her chair, her fingers twisting in her lap, her gaze fixed upon that small, impersonal microphone, which was capable of so terrifying a power.

It seemed only seconds before her turn came and Norman introduced her as a guide from the Tour Service of the UN. This was it. She leaned toward the mike and began to speak in a voice with a tremor in it. She couldn't forget herself or the microphone as Norman had urged her to do, but the story began somehow to tell itself. And then without warning she was caught up in the meaning of what she was saying, as always happened when she told these stories on the tour in ECOSOC. Her voice steadied and took on an earnestness that was more compelling than she knew. Now her heart was in her words and the simple telling came easily.

When she was through and Norman took over to introduce the next part of the program, she glanced toward the control room and saw Dave waving clasped hands at her in congratulation. Dave knew she was Reid Somers's daughter and that she was scared.

She hardly heard the rest of the half-hour program because of her relief at having the ordeal behind her. When Norman was through, he gave her a smile and a nod of approval and she felt that she'd not done so badly after all.

As mingled elation and relief swept through her, she began to wish that she had let Dad and Mother know about this, so they could have listened. But that had been too great a risk to take ahead of time.

After the broadcast Norman saw them home. On the way he told the children they had been fine, but he seemed to have a look of special meaning for Lisa as he spoke the words.

He came up to the apartment with her and they stepped in to find the phone ringing.

"Washington calling Miss Lisa Somers," the operator said.

She was startled. Had someone at home just by chance tuned in?

"Hello, Lisa," her father's voice said. "That was a fine job you did on the air this afternoon. You were a bit wavery at first, but when you hit your stride you were tops!"

She gasped a faint, "How did you know I was on?"

He chuckled. "Not because my daughter let me know, I'll admit. Your announcer on the program dropped us a card. Thank him, will you, and tell him we think he's good."

Lisa blinked at Norman, who was pretending to be reading a magazine across the room. Then her mother's voice came on from the extension at home and they had a brief three-way conversation before her parents hung up.

Lisa turned from the phone, her eyes bright, and Norman looked up from his magazine.

"I gather they liked you," he said.

"They did!" she cried, hugging herself the way Bunny sometimes did. "But you took a terrible risk. I'd have died if they heard me and I was awful."

He surprised her then. Until this moment he had approved impersonally, but now he dropped his pretense of standing aside. He crossed the room and took her hands warmly in his.

"I *knew* how good you'd be, Lisa! I was fairly popping with pride over there at the studio. Do you think for a minute that I could have kept this to myself and not let your parents know?"

It was wonderful to have him openly proud of her. She was happy to repeat what her father had said, and he looked more pleased than ever.

"Some day you'll have to meet my father," she said.

"There's nothing I'd like better. Well, I'll be running along now." But he hesitated as if he were a little uncertain. "Lisa – would you care to visit my home in Connecticut sometime? Arden, my stepmother, has invited me up and she says to bring someone along. It looks as if next Sunday will be a good time. Would you care to go?"

A fleeting question about Reland crossed her mind. But this invitation added one more touch to her feeling of happiness and she put the thought of Reland away. She wanted to visit his home more than anything, though she wasn't sure how it could be managed.

"I work on Sundays," she reminded him. "I haven't been here long enough to get the week end off."

"One of the other girls might trade with you," he suggested. "I'm sure you could manage it just this once."

"I'll try," she said. "I'd love to go."

She went to the door with him, thanking him for his help in putting the program across.

When Margie came home she wanted to hear all about the broadcast. Lisa told her,

204

keyed up still and ready to bubble over. She even told her about the possible date to visit Norman's home in Connecticut on Sunday, if she could get away.

This seemed more important to Margie than the rest. "That for Reland and her rebound!" she cried. "When you get invited to a fellow's home, it means you have an inside track, Lisa."

"But I'm not trying to marry Norman," Lisa said mildly.

"Why not? You could do worse." Margie headed for the kitchen and began to run water over potatoes in a pan. "I expect I shall probably marry Jimmy. Though of course he doesn't know about it yet. He suits me exactly."

Lisa, taking plates from the cupboard, paused and stared at her. "You don't even know him. Not really."

"Yes, I do. As well as I ever will. And he's for me."

Jimmy, Lisa suspected, was a cooked goose. From Margie's point of view life was pretty uncomplicated.

Margie left the subject of Jimmy as abruptly as she'd brought it up. "How about getting in some of your friends to help on this Halloween thing? Maybe Jeanie and Asha would loan Bunny and Carol and me some costumes. And maybe some of the girls would even help spell the mothers by going around with the kids."

"I'll see what I can manage," Lisa promised.

The next day she brought up the matter in the guides' lounge. Jeanie said she had a dress Carol might wear, and Asha offered, not only a sari, but instructions on wearing one. It was Reland, though, who surprised Lisa most by promising to help in taking around a group of children.

The matter of getting Sunday off was also arranged, so Lisa was set for her date to visit Norman's home.

14.   *Jaunt to Connecticut*

Sunday morning was bright and sunny, but there was a real nip in the air and a tingling wind that whipped color into cheeks. As the train left New York and began to roll through the suburban countryside, Lisa could see flaring autumn colors everywhere. It was nice to get away from stone and steel for a while and see growing things.

Norman seemed cheerful today and happy that she was able to come. But before long he was talking about Reland. She enjoyed the evening at Lisa's, he said, and he thought it had been good for her.

"Reland doesn't give herself enough chance to forget what happened," he said, "so this was the sort of thing she needs. She told me especially how much she liked meeting your mother."

"We enjoyed having her." Lisa watched the flying countryside thoughtfully. She couldn't help remembering her mother's words and Margie's, couldn't help wondering if, more than Norman suspected, Reland was finding a substitute for what she had lost. But she had not come out today to talk about Reland.

"Tell me about your home," she said, as the train drew to a stop at a small station along the way. "I know you lost your mother when you were rather young and that Arden is your stepmother. But that's all I do know. What's your father like?"

Norman hesitated, as if he searched for words. "Dad won't be there today. He's in the Midwest on business. Arden's quite a bit younger than he is and I think she gets lonely sometimes when he's away on trips. She likes to have me come up."

This didn't tell her much, but Lisa felt she could ask no more at the moment. When they reached Norman's town they took a taxi and drove through quiet Sunday streets, arched with the interlacing branches of old trees. Lisa was unprepared for the wide grounds of Norman's home, or for the big white house that had been built in the days of great families and great fortunes.

Arden came running downstairs to greet them – a slender young woman with short hair as fair as Margie's, very pretty and obviously delighted to see Norman. She kissed him affectionately, then turned to hold out a welcoming hand to Lisa.

"I'm so glad you could come. Norman wrote about how hard it was for you to get away on Sunday. Come upstairs and take off your things."

Arden ran lightly ahead, looking very attractive in her pale green frock and high-heeled brown pumps. But when she led Lisa into a bright bedroom with yards of white organdy curtain draped over the windows, Lisa noted that her face, without its smile, wore an anxious look. And there was a slight twitch that caught a muscle at the corner of her mouth now and then. But she was warm and friendly and seemed almost as young as Lisa herself, though she must have been fifteen years older.

"Here, I'll hang up your coat," Arden said. "And there's a dressing table near the window

208

where you can powder your nose. I *am* glad you're here. I'm always scolding Norman about not coming home oftener, and it's more fun for him if he can bring someone along."

Arden was not at all her preconceived notion of a stepmother, Lisa thought as she sat before the mirror and took out her compact. Behind her she was aware of Arden's bright, curious gaze and again the little twitch that disfigured her mouth. Her readiness to chatter was an indication of the loneliness Norman had mentioned.

"How nice to be a guide at the UN," she ran on. "I wish *I* could do something like that. But I know I'd never be smart enough. I wasn't even a very good steno in the days when I had a job. That's how I met Norman's father, you know. I guess he married me so I wouldn't mix up his letters any more."

Her laughter was quick, nervous, and once she went to the door and listened with an air that was plainly uneasy.

"What a lovely place you have," Lisa said. She turned toward a window to look out at broad lawns and a clump of willow trees where the ground dipped toward a stream.

"It is lovely," Arden agreed. "But I'm more used to the city. Of course this place has been in the family for generations and

209

Lewis is very proud of it. Come along, if you're ready."

They went out into the hall, but as they approached the stairs Norman called from the doorway of another room.

"Want to see where I grew up, Lisa?" he asked.

Arden motioned to her to go look and Lisa went into the smaller bedroom where airplanes decorated the wallpaper. It was plainly a boy's room, with a narrow bed and severe gray spread. A maple desk stood near a window and there was a long bookshelf against one wall. On the desk was a much-thumbed globe and Norman reached out to spin it affectionately.

"You can see I practically wore it through as a kid, poking at all the places in the world that I wanted to see when I grew up. They're still there, but I'll catch up with some of them yet."

"Of course you will," Lisa said. She saw a photograph in a silver frame on the high dresser and moved closer to look at it.

"My mother," said Norman. "Her name was Elizabeth McIntosh."

The woman in the picture had been older than Arden when the photograph was taken, but where Arden was merely pretty, Elizabeth was beautiful. Her brow was wide and her dark eyes looked out at you with interest and kindliness. Nevertheless, her face was not a happy one.

Arden waited for them at the top of the stairs and when they joined her she spoke quickly. "Norman, your father is going to be home after all. I had a wire from him this morning. His plane should be in by now, so he's probably on the way here."

It seemed to Lisa that there was a momentary stiffening on Norman's part. Then he said cheerfully, "That's fine, Arden. I haven't seen him for quite a while. Now Lisa can meet him too."

They went down to the beautifully furnished living room and Lisa was aware that a moment of crisis for Arden had passed. A great fireplace at one end of the room, where a fire danced behind brass andirons, drew Lisa. She went to it and held out her hands, though she wasn't in the least cold.

"How lovely to have a real fireplace! Never in all my life have I lived in a house with a fireplace. Mother never had much time for the housekeeping that a place like this would need. But I've always thought it would be wonderful to live in a real house instead of an apartment and stay there forever."

"Norman couldn't wait till he grew up and got away," Arden said ruefully.

211

There was affection in the look Norman turned upon Arden. "That wasn't your fault."

A maid came to the door just then and Arden shook her head. "Tell Cook we'll have to hold dinner until Mr. Bond gets here. It shouldn't be long now. Henry is driving him home from the airport."

Norman had gone to a window and Arden went over to him. Lisa pretended a continued interest in the dancing flames, trying not to hear what they were saying. But Arden's voice rose nervously and her words were plain.

"He'll be tired when he gets here. He does work awfully hard, you know, Norman. So don't argue with him about anything. Don't make him angry."

"I'll do my best," Norman promised in a low tone, and they came to join Lisa in chairs around the fire.

A little later there was the sound of a car in the driveway, the slam of a car door. The maid hurried to open the front door. Arden gave Norman a last look of appeal and ran into the hall.

"Let's stay put," Norman said. "He'll go upstairs first before he comes in here. You might as well know how things are. I'm sorry he's home. I wouldn't be here if I'd expected him. I can't guarantee whether he'll be civil to you or not. I've never forgiven him for

212

the way he talked to Reland one time, just because he's prejudiced against the British. But if it gets bad we'll leave."

"Oh no!" Lisa said quickly. "I wouldn't want to make it hard for Arden. She's very sweet." So Reland had been here.

"She's better than he deserves," Norman said shortly. "And you're right, of course. Just don't let him scare you. He enjoys flattening people."

Arden rejoined them, her cheeks pink and her eyes bright. "Things went well on the trip," she told them. "He's in a good mood."

Norman looked skeptical, while Lisa smiled reassuringly at Arden. She was quite certain that Norman's father was not going to "scare" her.

A few moments later he came into the room – a big man, with a pinkish complexion and shaggy eyebrows that gave him a scowling look. His jaw was square and his straight, unsmiling mouth did not change when he saw his son.

"So that's how it is," Mr. Bond said gruffly. "You come to the house only when I'm not home."

Norman grinned as if at a good joke. "That's right, Dad. Saves a lot of wear and tear on both of us. Dad, this is Lisa Somers, a friend of mine."

213

Lisa couldn't remember when anyone had looked at her with so complete a lack of interest. Mr. Bond acknowledged the introduction, glanced at her briefly, and then asked Arden when dinner would be ready.

It was ready at once and they went into a moss-green dining room, with pale willow fronds in the wallpaper, and still another fireplace.

"You sit here, Lisa, where you can see the fire," Arden said, and put Norman across the table from her.

It was a lovely, gracious room, and yet in the presence of the man who sat at the head of the table Lisa hardly dared enjoy it.

"You're looking fit, Dad," Norman said over the soup. "Did the trip go well?"

Mr. Bond launched into a discussion of machinery performance and Midwestern contracts that meant little to Lisa. As she spooned her soup, she maintained a polite expression of attention, and was startled when Mr. Bond halted his words suddenly to stare at his son.

"I'm sure this interests you," he said with heavy sarcasm. Then he turned with equal suddenness to Lisa. "Young lady, what do you think of a fellow who could have stepped into the board of directors of one of the most successful machinery manufacturing companies in the country, and who threw it all over to work in radio? *Radio!*" He seemed to spread the word with vitriol as he spoke it.

Lisa managed a smile and summoned the nearest cliché to help her out. "I suppose it takes all sorts of people and all sorts of jobs —"

"Oyster stuffing!" Mr. Bond muttered, staring at the platter which had been set before him.

For a second Lisa thought the remark was addressed to her. Then she saw the muscle twitch at the corner of Arden's mouth.

"We didn't know in time that you would be here, Lewis," Arden said gently. "I'm terribly sorry —"

Mr. Bond served grumpily, while Arden and Norman did their best to carry off the dinner with some air of social grace. Lisa helped when she could, but there was no escaping the fact that Norman's father had put a constraint on them all. He seemed to take satisfaction in his own bad manners and lack of consideration — as if he had arrived at a position where he could do exactly as he pleased without suffering the consequences.

Now he ate in silence, except for an occasional "Humph!" But over a second helping he stared once more at Lisa, his eyebrows drawing together like a line of fur across his forehead.

"I suppose you have a job, young lady? Where do you work?"

"I'm a tour guide for the United Nations," Lisa told him.

Mr. Bond stared. "Another one! Not much future there, I should think."

Lisa tried to explain. "It isn't supposed to be a career job. They don't want us to stay on more than two years at the most. But it may be a stepping stone to something I want to do."

"No more future than the old League of Nations," Mr. Bond went on, as if she had not spoken. "If America had any sense we'd pull out and tend to our own affairs instead of trying to feed the world and support a lot of goldbrickers who are too lazy to work."

Lisa opened her mouth for a hot retort, and then closed it. She was here as Arden's guest and she couldn't make things worse for her hostess. She knew her cheeks were warm and she stole a look at Norman to see how he had reacted to his father's words.

There was a bright look in Norman's eyes. "I suppose you know, Dad," he drawled, "that you're talking to Reid Somers's daughter."

For a moment Lewis Bond looked as if he might explode. He stared at Lisa as if she had turned into a rattlesnake at his own table. His

216

opinion of her father was plain to see.

"Of all the dangerous flapdoodle that goes out on the air –" he began.

This time she didn't wait for him to finish. "Don't you think it will be a lot more dangerous if the nations don't start working together? We can't stand separate any more and live. What happens to a man in Indonesia affects our lives right here in America."

"Not mine, it doesn't!" said Mr. Bond. "We can take care of ourselves within our own borders. We don't need the rest of the world."

"Okay, Dad, okay," Norman said soothingly. "You're only living back in the fourteenth century. We have airplanes today – remember?"

Arden gasped and started to chatter about what a lovely fall it had been, but Mr. Bond squelched her with a look and proceeded to take Reid Somers and his theories apart, bit by bit. Lisa drew a deep breath and made herself relax. She glanced at Norman and gave a quick shake of her head to prevent his interference. When Mr. Bond wound along to the end of his diatribe she managed a smile.

"How long has this house been in your family, Mr. Bond?" she asked. "It must be quite old."

Norman suppressed a chuckle and Mr.

Bond blinked uncertainly. Obviously he hated to leave his topic, but on the other hand Lisa had touched on something that appealed to him.

All through dessert she learned about the house. Apparently it had once belonged to another branch of the family, though Lewis Bond had grown up here as a boy, raised by an elderly aunt. It was not left to him when his aunt died, but he bought it about twenty-five years ago. Listening, Lisa could see what this house meant to him. It must have been a final symbol of the success he had achieved. Its beauty and grace meant little, but owning it put him in the position of crowing over the rest of the family which had once snubbed him and regarded him as a poor relation.

When the uncomfortable meal was over, Mr. Bond said he had some work to do and went off to his study. Arden was ready to burst into tears but Lisa managed to tell some funny stories about the tour service as they sat around the fire again. Yet the day had been spoiled, and Norman found an excuse before long to get them away.

Arden said, "I'll drive you to the train." They got into their coats and left the house without disturbing Mr. Bond. At the station they sat in the car for a few minutes and

Arden begged Lisa to come again. "You must bring her another time, Norman. I'd love to have her." She went on to make futile little apologies for her husband and Lisa sensed that in spite of everything Arden loved him and looked up to him.

"I don't know when I can come out again," she said, "since I work on Sundays. But the next time you're in town, why not come over to the United Nations and have lunch with me? It would be nice to see you again."

Arden looked so pleased that Lisa was aware once more of her loneliness. Norman, however, lapsed into a gloomy silence that he did not break even when they were on the train heading back to Manhattan.

Once Lisa spoke to him lightly. "Don't mind. Some people are like that and there isn't any use arguing with them. It's an emotional thing and unless you get them to change their basic feelings, no amount of reasoning does any good. Your father must have had a pretty unhappy childhood, didn't he? And now he's trying to pay off the world."

Norman nodded. "Yes, I suppose he has that much excuse. His aunt didn't like children and didn't want the job of raising him. But I can't forgive him everything he does because of that. Other people have

219

unhappy childhoods and grow up with some ability to see the other fellow's side. He's like a – a steamroller, Lisa. He flattens everything around him. He couldn't quite flatten my mother because she was a strong person, but he made her bitterly unhappy. What I remember most about my childhood is the ugly quarrels between them. And now he's flattening poor little Arden."

"I can see why you left," Lisa said, her sympathy going out to him, though there was so little she could say.

Norman's mouth was tight and straight. "He'd have flattened me too. The strange thing is that both my mother and Arden should care so much about him. That's why he could make them unhappy." He stared out the train window. "It was worse for my mother than it is for Arden because she was a brilliant person who might have been somebody in her own right."

Lisa listened, thinking of how different was the marriage of her own parents. Each was happily dependent on the other and there was no contest between them, no effort on the part of one to dominate the other.

"I'm glad you didn't let the things Dad said upset you," Norman went on. "Just the same, I wouldn't have asked you out today if I'd expected him to be there. It was pretty awful the time I brought Reland."

They did not speak of his father again, and Lisa talked of matters that might catch his attention and make him forget this visit. When he left her at the apartment he held her hand for just a moment. "Thanks for being such a good sport," he said.

She went inside with a sense of pleasure and elation. In spite of everything, she had a feeling that the day had gone well.

15. Trick or Treat

Halloween fell on Reland's day off and she came over to help the Starling children dress. Margie had to work, but promised to spell Reland in taking a group around in the evening. While Lisa could not be on hand for the dress-up part, she heard the details later on.

Jeanie Soong had loaned Carol the costume of a modern Chinese lady – a long blue tunic dress with a high collar and slit skirt. Bunny, who had taken lessons from Asha in sari draping, looked fine in a brightly dyed cotton sari Asha had loaned her. That is, she looked fine until she moved.

Then, regardless of preliminary practice, she clutched ungracefully at the folds and seemed at every step about to lose her draperies. Not that this daunted her in the least. She galloped about, clutching at her scarf and tripping over her mother's slip, which served as a long gown beneath the sari. In the center of her forehead she had painted a smudgy caste mark with Beth's lipstick.

Mimi, who already owned a pleated skirt of doubtful tartan, was considered to represent Scotland. Reland brought over a tartan scarf to drap across Mimi's shoulder as the Scotsman wore his plaid. The fact that the two tartans did not match, troubled no one but Reland, who shuddered to think what a confused version of the Scottish costume Mimi displayed.

"Never mind, Reland," Bunny told her sympathetically. "We're supposed to represent the United Nations, aren't we? So the more mixed up we are the better."

"Mixed up" was certainly the phrase for the national, international and semi-national costumes in which the children turned out to confound the neighbors all afternoon and evening. But the plan had been well publicized, thanks to Norman's broadcast, the efforts of the mothers' club, and Bunny's own energetic campaign. So doors were opened readily and coins clinked into the yellow-banded milk cartons.

The monster, as Lisa was informed when she came home to dinner, was dressed up as a real Chinese dragon, green and happy. When they went to a place where people were reluctant about making a contribution to the Children's Fund, he breathed fire and scared them plenty, Bunny reported. He was the Trick part of the organization.

But by the time Lisa learned all this, the milk cartons were already jingling with coins and the children were coming home tired but happy for a quick supper before they went out on their rounds again. Bunny had broken the gang into groups to cover separate parts of the neighborhood, and a volunteer adult was in charge of each squad. Of course the grownups stood back and let the children step up to the doors, displaying their pumpkin-yellow tags as they explained about the Children's Fund. Lisa turned the Mexican pig bank upside down and shook Pedro free of his treasure for her own contribution to the Fund.

She warmed dinner up hastily out of cans so that Margie could be ready to go out with the children. Reland admitted to aching feet and stayed home with Lisa, perching on the kitchen stool while dishes were done. Tonight she looked happier than Lisa had ever seen her. She had joined in the fun of helping the children and had won them all with her endearing gentleness and her ready sympathy.

"Norman is going to drop by for me later in the evening," she told Lisa. "He wanted to get in on some of these Halloween doings himself, but a broadcast was in the making, so he had to stay with it."

Lisa swished suds in the dishpan. She had walked on air a bit since Sunday, and she wanted to hold to the pleasant feeling of a rosy world that centered about Norman. But now the earth was there beneath her feet and it jolted her a little to feel it.

The choice between them was Norman's, she told herself again. If there were a choice. He could, of course, like them equally well and be serious about neither. But somehow she felt that would not be the case. He had *begun* to make a choice, just as she had begun. If only a little, each had turned to the other. Yet here was Reland with the sadness falling away from her and tonight Norman was calling for her here. A casual gesture? How could she know?

"Norman told me about your trip to his father's house," Reland went on, picking up a glass from the sink and polishing it to a shine. "Of course I can never go out there again when Mr. Bond is home. What happened was quite terrible."

"Oh," said Lisa, adding more soap powder than she needed. She would ask no questions. She didn't want to know.

"Norman says you kept your head." Reland sounded wistful. "You didn't let yourself get upset. But his father behaved quite dreadfully to me. He is the sort of American who goes abroad and gives all the rest of you a bad name. I felt sorry for Norman, but at the same time I couldn't accept what his father said when he started talking about 'you English.' I explained that I was Scottish, not English, and that he could call me British if he wanted to be correct. But in any event, what he was saying didn't apply to any of us."

Lisa could understand that Mr. Bond would never see or care about such a distinction.

"I don't think he even heard me." Reland held up a second glass and studied it. "He went on telling me how much he disapproved of the English, when obviously he knew nothing about them. He was still fighting your War of Independence, I think. As you can imagine, it was pretty bleak. I tried to answer him, but I only disgraced myself by crying."

"I know how you felt," Lisa said. "But you mustn't mind. Mr. Bond doesn't represent most of America."

"I couldn't help being upset. Even though I know Norman hates scenes. I suppose he grew up with so many of them. He was quiet all the way home on the train and I knew he was sorry he'd brought me there. I was quite frightened."

But Reland did not look frightened. She was smiling as if her thoughts were pleasant ones. Lisa felt so sharp and sudden a twinge of jealousy that it took her by surprise. For all of a minute she disliked Reland with violent intensity. The sensation was shaking. It made her feel a little ill. She managed to thrust it away and steady herself. Reland did not deserve her dislike. She had been through enough.

"I can tell you," Reland went on, "that I worried for a while until he got over it. I don't know what I'd do without Norman. Sometimes he reminds me a little of Phil – the man I was engaged to at home. He has the same way of taking me in hand and making me believe I'm more courageous and clever and – more everything than I am."

"Don't run yourself down," Lisa said. Then, knowing she sounded stiff, she tried to soften her words. "Everyone likes you, Reland, and admires you."

Reland looked at her with eyes that were

trustingly eager. "You're sweet to say that, Lisa."

Lisa busied herself putting away the dishpan, swishing out the sink with clean water. She hung up the dish towel with a flick of distaste, as if she were ridding herself of an uncomfortable subject. "Let's go back to the living room."

Reland went ahead through the door and settled down in a chair near the windows. "Sometimes I seem to get quivery with feelings I don't want. Like one of those sensitive plants that curl up if you so much as touch them. It's hard not to be that way. One minute you're safe and everything is marvelous. And then lightning strikes and you're done for. Everything is over."

Lisa ached for her a little, knowing what she meant. "You're too young to talk like that," she said. She wanted to put up some barrier between Reland and herself; Reland, who sat there looking trustful as a child one could never betray.

"I'm sorry." Reland spoke softly. "I've made you impatient with me. I've no business chattering like this."

Lisa was grateful for the ringing of the doorbell which made it unnecessary to answer. She hurried to open the door. Norman came in smiling and greeted both girls without any trace of self-consciousness.

"I ran into Bunny and company on the sidewalk," he said. "Margie tried to save me, but I didn't stand a chance. I had to turn my pockets inside out. I gather the whole thing is a huge success – which brings me to some plans I want to talk over with both you girls. You first, Lisa."

Lisa sat where the lamplight would not fall too brightly upon her. Let Reland sit in the light, looking lovely and wistful. Lisa wanted shadows so her thoughts could not be too easily read. Norman talked on and she watched, liking the mood of excitement that touched him as he warmed to the idea he was explaining. Liking the way his hair grew back from his forehead, with one lock that escaped and fell forward. Liking his hands and the way he moved them – not in idle gesture, but strongly, with purpose. It was hard to listen, because of watching him.

This idea, he explained, grew out of a talk he had this week with Mrs. Schermer, who handled public relations matters for UNICEF. She had heard Lisa and the children on the recent radio program and was enthusiastic about what they had done. Since arrangements had been made for children from two out-of-town communities to come in next Saturday and deliver their Halloween collections in person, Mrs. Schermer thought it might be fun if Lisa's group came over too.

Lisa stopped watching Norman. When she stared at the carpet, she could make herself listen.

"It's going to be quite a show," he went on. "I'm vice president in charge of candy bars, among other things. And of course it's good for wonderful publicity in the papers to help the UNICEF cause. What we're trying for now is a television hookup that will give a real picture of the event. The bank up on the cafeteria floor is getting in a special counting machine to take care of all the pennies and dimes. It should make some good television shots."

"Surely children from all over the country don't send in *pennies!*" Reland cried.

"Some of them did in the beginning," Norman said. "But now groups working on the project are asked to send checks. This will be a special occasion, however, and that rule won't hold. The point is this, Lisa – Mrs. Schermer would like you to come over and interview some of the children about their adventures in collecting. On television, of course. Will you do it?"

She so wanted to please him. But not this way. She had managed to get through on radio without disgracing herself, but she

229

couldn't risk it again. She shook her head unhappily. "Television's worse than radio. This sort of thing isn't for me."

"I thought you were over those notions," Norman said.

"Why can't you do it?" Lisa asked him. "After all, you're the experienced announcer."

"Oh, I'll be there to cover the event. But Mrs. Schermer wants you for the interview. She mentioned that especially. For one thing you're prettier than I am. And the guide uniform will go over well on television. You're not really scared, are you?"

"Lisa, you'll be wonderful!" Reland leaned forward, her chin in her hands. "I can just see –"

"Not scared – petrified," Lisa said.

"But you grew up in a radio family." Reland was puzzled. "I should think you'd be accustomed to that sort of thing."

"Everyone has moments of nervousness," Norman said, "but most of us do a better job if we worry ahead of time. Then we rise to the occasion. You'll do just as beautifully as you did the other day. And this time it's even more important."

He waited for her answer. Lisa got up restlessly and went to the window to look down at the street. The sound of children's voices came to her and she could see a costumed group in the light of a street lamp. Their UNICEF tags shone bright yellow.

Reland suddenly took her side. "Perhaps, after all, you shouldn't ask her to do this, Norman. I can remember nearly dying the first few times I took out a tour. You just don't understand the way we feel because you're not like that."

Unreasonably, Lisa stiffened. She didn't want Reland to plead her case. Abruptly she turned from the window. "All right. I'll do it."

Norman's look was personal, for her only, and it approved her words. "Of course you will. Now that's taken care of, we need you too, Reland."

"You do?" said Reland, looking pleased as a kitten that has just been stroked. "But what can I do?"

"Help with the children, so I won't be completely mobbed. You're especially good with kids."

Reland nodded. "I grew up in a big family. And of course I'll love helping if there's something I can do. This is going to be fun, Lisa."

Lisa smiled, but she was disliking Reland again, and hating the feeling, so quick to rise, so unreasonable. It would be good for

Reland to help. This was just the sort of thing she needed. But how easily Norman walked between them. Equidistant from each. If he took a step toward one, there followed a step toward the other, quickly, surely. He was playing no favorites. He liked them both.

The Halloween groups began to straggle in now, their costumes somewhat bedraggled, though spirits were high. The building's corridors were noisy that night, but no one hushed the children as the money was sorted into nickels, dimes, quarters, even some dollar bills. Bunny's crusade had served the Children's Fund well.

Before the final pennies were counted, Norman took Reland home and Lisa had no words with him alone.

On the following Saturday Lisa and Reland were released for special duty. Television cameras were set up to catch shots of the children as they swarmed into the lobby. The sound track picked up something of the roar, and the "Ohs!" of astonishment as the young visitors beheld the beauty of the UN buildings for the first time.

It was too noisy in the lobby for interviews, but there were further shots taken upstairs when the counting machine went to work and Reland put groups of children through to watch in delight and wonder. One flight further up were lounges and meeting rooms, where an on-the-spot interview could be held. Lisa had a feeling that with these children almost anything could happen. She came armed with questions she meant to ask, but when Norman introduced her and set Bunny before her, the old freezing terror returned and every question fled from her mind.

There might have been an awkward moment if Bunny, who showed no concern about cameras and microphones, hadn't plunged into her own line of questioning concerning the tour guides. How, for instance, did you keep that blue cord from falling off their shoulders? Norman laughed and said, "Just which young lady is interviewing which young lady?" and Lisa recovered her wits.

Once she got into the swing of the thing she began to enjoy herself. She questioned one child after another and got an ad-lib show that held a few surprises, since the children were unpredictable. Now and then Norman stepped in to help, and after it was over and the children had gone, leaving the United Nations buildings surprisingly empty and quiet, Lisa dropped into a chair and closed her eyes. She had no idea how the program had gone and could only feel limp relief that it was over.

"Lisa," Norman said in quiet approval, "you might as well face it and get used to it – you're really good at this sort of thing. I suspected it the first time, and now I know. This show will be on film, as well as live, so it can be rebroadcast abroad. You're going to be practically famous. Remember, I was the first to tell you that you've got a future ahead of you in radio and television, if you want it."

Lisa opened her eyes. "I don't want it! I've proved what I needed to prove for the sake of my own self-respect. But I don't want to be another Reid Somers. I want to be me and I *don't* want to work in radio!"

"I hope you don't really mean that," said a woman's voice from the doorway and Lisa looked up at Mrs. Schermer.

Lisa nodded fervently. "Norman won't believe me, but I do mean it."

"Will you come upstairs to see me one of these days when you're free?" Mrs. Schermer asked. "Just for a little talk?"

"Why yes – I'd be glad to," Lisa said, but she stared at the doorway blankly when Mrs. Schermer had gone. "Why do you suppose she wants to see me?" she asked Norman.

"The opening of a door, Miss Somers," he told her. "Maybe."

But Lisa had no intention of going through any door that had to do with radio. It was fine not to have disgraced herself. But she wanted no more of this sort of nervous strain. This was no life work for her. She'd proved herself twice and that was enough. Mrs. Schermer's invitation had been issued casually – it probably meant nothing. And so in the weeks that followed she did nothing about it.

Once she was asked to be a guest speaker at an assembly in a school auditorium to talk to the children about the UN. The Department of Public Information granted permission to give the talk, and she loved doing it. It was just a different form of a guided tour. She talked about the Children's Fund, but she made no connection in her mind with UNICEF until Mrs. Schermer dropped her a note of thanks for the good job she had done at the school.

Lisa was surprised, but by now she had more personal things to think about. November was gone and the early part of December was flying by – the rush season of the UN. Occasionally she went out with Norman, but she knew he dated Reland too. She enjoyed her dates with him, and he seemed to enjoy being with her. In fact, she enjoyed them so much that now and then she soberly considered not going out with him any more. But what excuse could she give him? She could hardly say, "I'm beginning to like you too much." There seemed to be no reasonable way out and so the occasional dates went on and she tried not to look forward to them too much.

In mid-December Arden, Norman's stepmother, phoned the apartment to invite her to Connecticut for dinner Christmas day, but Lisa thanked her and refused for the very good reason that she was going home to Washington for three whole days.

16.   High and Low

One day shortly before Christmas Lisa, poking around in a Greenwich Village shop looking for gift ideas, came upon an original water color. The painting showed a broadcast studio with an interviewer and two flustered lady guests at a table microphone. Part of the control booth window was visible, with the show's director watching and the engineer at his control panels. The scene was delightfully satirized and Lisa knew she had to have it for Norman.

The price was a little more than she meant to spend, but she couldn't resist. She carried the framed water color home, done up in brown paper, happy in her anticipation of Norman's pleasure.

By the day before Christmas, brown paper had given away to holiday green, sprinkled with silver stars and tied with a tinsel bow and a sprig of holly. Norman took her to the train when she left for Washington, and while they waited in the glass-roofed section of the train shed, she gave him the package. He whistled in admiration at the wrappings and tucked it under his arm. Then, fumbling through coat pockets as if he had misplaced something, he produced a long narrow box done in wrappings as handsome as her own.

"I'll have you know," he said, "that I wrapped and tied this myself. When I was in school I worked as a package wrapper Saturdays in a department store. So it's a professional job."

The brown gift paper was sprinkled with pine cones, and tied with a huge gold bow, elaborately looped. Lisa accepted the package with pleased anticipation.

"I can't decide whether to keep it and open it with the family when we look at our presents tomorrow morning," she pondered. "Or –"

Norman settled the matter. "Let's open these two now. I was never any good at waiting. And if it wasn't for Arden, Christmas wouldn't be much at home."

"All right," Lisa agreed. "After all, this is practically Christmas Eve."

Over a loudspeaker in the station singers were caroling, "Deck the halls..." and around them crowds waited, laden with packages and boxes. There were holly pins on women's lapels and a feeling of Christmas excitement in the air.

Norman drew Lisa away from the crowd and they found a quiet spot near a row of locker boxes.

"You first," he said.

She opened her package, slipping the handsome golden bow off carefully in order to save it. There was a strip of brightly colored silk, folded into the box. She pulled it out and it fell into a big square scarf. The center was blue, with the familiar wreath and world of the UN emblem, and all around the border were the flags of the Member nations in their bright red and green and yellow. It was a lovely thing and she knew he must have looked long to find something so exactly right.

She folded the soft stuff about her neck so it would show at the open collar of her navy-blue coat. A nearby gum machine presented a mirror and she stepped before it to get the effect. The scarf at her throat was brightly beautiful. She turned back to Norman, her eyes shining.

"What a perfect gift! Thank you!"

He looked pleased as he turned to his own package and unwrapped it. When he saw the painting he laughed out loud in delight.

"Up it goes on the wall in my place," he said. "Jimmy will like it too. Something to cheer us both after a hard day."

Now a portion of the crowd in the station was surging toward the gate where a sign had gone up announcing the train for Washington. The loud-speaker blared the stops and cried, "All aboard!"

Lisa turned toward the gate, but Norman drew her back, his hands clasped upon her elbows.

"Three days is a long time," he said. "Take care of yourself, Lisa. I'll miss you."

She couldn't help the way her heart went into her eyes, telling him more than she wanted to tell. He bent down and kissed her mouth. Not a gentle kiss, but one that was hard and almost angry. Then he let her go and picked up her suitcase and hurried her after the thinning crowd.

He did not speak again until he got her aboard the train and had lifted her bag to the rack above her head. "Have fun at home," he said, and was gone so quickly that she scarcely had time to say good-by.

She leaned back in the seat, only dimly aware of the holiday crowd around her, of the platform outside her window. When a man took the seat next to her and buried himself in a newspaper she was relieved because that meant she wouldn't have to make polite conversation with a stranger. She had brought a book along and she opened it, studied print on a cream-colored page. But she saw only Norman's face as he had looked down at her, the darkening gray of his eyes as he had bent to kiss her.

The train jerked and the station began to slide past, but she did not see it. Norman's kiss hadn't meant anything, she tried to tell herself. Any man might kiss a girl good-by if he took her to a train. But there was a warm happiness in her that denied all protests. He had stepped across the line to her side, and he could not easily go back.

Three days and she would see him again. She would miss Christmas with him, but New Year's Eve was still ahead. He had made no plans, but that was like him. His dates were apt to be on sudden impulse, and when she had other arrangements and couldn't change, he never seemed to mind. Yet he never planned any sooner for the next time. So a New Year's Eve date seemed likely.

She tried to push away the thought of Reland. Would he be with her on Christmas Day? No matter. It was New Year's Eve that counted, greeting the new year together. She was the girl he had kissed, and he would miss her while she was gone.

Christmas at home was more fun than ever. There was an increased warmth of affection because this was the first time a member of the family had been away for so long, and it was lovely to be together again. Her father exclaimed about how well she looked, but her mother's gaze saw more than he did, with quick intuition. Mother asked no questions, however, and Lisa offered no confidences. Always before she had been ready to talk to her mother about any boy who interested her. But this time a shyness held her back, and a feeling that this was something she could not yet share. It was too nebulous and uncertain. If it came to nothing, she wanted no one to know.

In some strange way she found the world about her subtly changed. It was as if she saw everything more intensely now, as if all the colors were brighter, the sounds clearer. Norman was never long out of her thoughts, and every small thing that happened was something to save to tell him about. It was like living all experience twice — once when it happened and again when she could tell Norman.

One day her father asked about the young man who had been with her on both radio and television shows as announcer. She talked about Norman then with a carefully casual air, hugging her secret to herself.

"Promising young fellow," her father said. "Good voice. Good personality. He should go places if he stays with his job."

She stored his words away to repeat to Norman later. He would appreciate such praise from Reid Somers, and she loved her father all the more for giving it.

One evening Dad read aloud a few chapters of his UN book and Lisa found that he listened to her comments with a new respect, as if her work made her something of an authority in the very field he was writing about. It was a novel sensation to be treated as more than a little girl by her father and she enjoyed it.

The holidays flew by – there was so much to talk about, so much to do. Yet there were times when it seemed forever before she was back on the train for New York. She wished now that she had told Norman when she was returning so he could have met her at the station. But he had not thought to ask and she had not mentioned the matter.

She reached home to find Margie in a state bordering on delirium. During November and December Margie had been dating Jimmy with a more than twice-a-week regularity.

"Jimmy has proposed!" she cried, flinging herself upon Lisa and whirling her wildly around the room. "Goodness, how hard I've had to work – but I managed it finally. He thinks it was all his own idea, and he even gave me time to consider his proposal. He didn't want to rush me – the darling dumb bunny! I considered for three whole minutes before I accepted him."

"You're a scheming woman," Lisa teased. "But you know I'm happy about this. Jimmy is nice and I think you're right for each other."

Margie let Lisa go and dropped into a chair, her laughter gone, her air suddenly tragic.

"What's the matter?" Lisa asked, startled by the swift change.

"It's so horrible to think I might never have met him. It was such a slim little chance. If you'd objected to popcorn I'd never have known him at all."

Lisa burst into laughter. "But then you wouldn't have known the difference so it would have been quite painless."

"Oh, no!" Margie said, clasping her hands over her heart. "I'd have known. I always

243

had a sort of hollow, waiting feeling until I met Jimmy. It's scary to think what a small chance it was."

As she carried her suitcase into the bedroom to unpack, Lisa sobered. It *was* a slim chance, when you stopped to think. By what a slim margin of luck had she come here to the UN and met Norman! And what an empty sort of world it would now seem without him. Realistically, she knew that sooner or later she'd have met someone else, but for the moment she could imagine no one but Norman. No one else could have been so *right*.

As Lisa unpacked, Margie spread out Christmas gifts for her to see. She and Lisa had exchanged packages before Lisa left and Margie said she loved wearing the pearl choker and earrings Lisa gave her. Margie's gift of an atomizer already graced Lisa's side of the dressing table. Now Margie showed her three presents from Jimmy – a box of miniature chocolates, a pink orlon sweater, and a bangle for her charm bracelet. On New Year's Eve, Margie said, she and Jimmy had a big date together. And that reminded her of something.

"Goodness! I forgot to tell you. Norman phoned a while ago. He wasn't sure when you'd be home. But he's going to call again in a little bit. Bet it's to date you for New

Year's Eve, Lisa. He sounded disappointed when you weren't here."

How nice of him to call so quickly, Lisa thought. She liked the inward flutter of anticipation at the thought of talking to him so soon. She felt almost like dancing around the room as Margie had done. Love certainly did queer giddy things to the equilibrium.

Unpacking, she came upon the bow of gold ribbon from Norman's present. Since he had tied it himself, it was part of his gift and she wouldn't throw it away for anything. Now she took Pedro, the Mexican pig, coin-poor since Halloween, and dressed him up in the golden bow. He looked so perky and festive that she carried him into the living room and set him on the radio cabinet to decorate the room. Margie had hung a holly wreath in the window and set out little wax candles on the sill – snowmen skating.

As Lisa stood back to admire Pedro, the telephone rang and she tried not to go for it too quickly.

The voice was Norman's and he sounded pleased to know she was back. He asked about her stay in Washington and how her family were, but she told him only a little. There was so much to say and she wanted to save it till they could really talk.

When there was a pause he said, "Lisa, I've

been wanting to tell you about New Year's Eve. I may not have a chance to see you at work, and –" he hesitated.

"Yes?" she said lightly. What else could there be to say except to arrange for their evening together?

"I'd like you to understand," he went on hesitantly. "I meant to tell you this at the station before you went to Washington. But then it seemed to be the wrong time. I – I won't be able to see you New Year's Eve, Lisa."

She couldn't quite believe his words. In her thoughts, leaping ahead so confidently, the date was settled.

"Why – that's all right," she heard herself say. He had some reason, of course. Some reason which she would understand and sympathize with as soon as he told her.

He went on gently and his kindness was harder to take than if he had been abrupt. "This is something we planned quite a while ago, Reland and I. Do you understand, Lisa? I wanted you to know in time so –"

"It's quite all right," she said quickly. "I have other plans."

She hated the sound of her own false words, but she had to say them quickly. She had to save something of her own sick pride.

"Lisa!" he said. "Don't be angry."

"I'm not angry," she told him. "Why should I be? Have a lovely time – you and Reland. And now, if you don't mind, I've some unpacking to do and I'm rather tired. Good-by."

She listened for his "Good-by" and then set the receiver down. Across the room Pedro stared at her from beneath his perky bow. She turned her back on him and went to her unpacking in silence, fighting the tears. Margie was solemnly putting away her gifts. When the silence grew long she sat on the edge of her bed and chewed thoughtfully on her pony tail.

"I couldn't help hearing," she said. "And if he's taking Reland out, he's just a – a stinker!"

"He has every right to take out anyone he pleases," Lisa said in a voice that cracked around the edges.

"Jimmy told me about the present you gave him," Margie said. "The picture. Norman put it up on the wall right away. But Reland gave him a picture too. One of herself. And he put that on his desk. Honestly, Lisa, I've a good mind to tell him a couple of things myself. Of all the –"

Lisa flung down a pair of shoes and went quickly to stand above her. "Don't you say one word! Not to Jimmy, or Norman, or anyone. Promise me, Margie."

"Oh, all right," said Margie. "Don't bite me. But if I were you, I wouldn't take this lying down. You let a man get away with that sort of thing, and the first thing you know he walks all over you. Let him make up his mind between you and Reland."

Lisa blew her nose hard. "I'm not lying down. I knew all along that Norman had to make his choice. Now he's made it. That's his right. I'm not wearing my heart on my sleeve."

"Atta baby!" Margie cried, but she looked worried.

When the lights were off and Lisa had wriggled down into bed, her brave words no longer shielded her. Wherever she kept her heart, this hurt. She knew now that his kiss had been a whim of the moment. Even at the time she had felt he didn't really want to kiss her. Perhaps he thought she expected it and wanted to send her off gaily to a happy Christmas. Her cheeks burned at the thought.

It had always been Reland. And why not? Reland was so pretty, so gentle, so much in need of love. How could any man resist her if she reached out to him? Lisa couldn't blame Norman, but only herself for being foolishly blind.

But she would not be blind again. And

Norman mustn't know he had hurt her. He must never, never guess.

17. *Gray January*

During the four days before New Year's Lisa saw Norman just twice. The first time, he was having lunch with Reland in the cafeteria. She managed to smile as she went by his table and his own greeting was friendly but casual. The second time she saw him coming toward her down a corridor. She wasn't sure of herself and turned aside into an empty conference room.

For an instant she almost hoped he would follow her, disturbing though it might be to talk to him. But he did not. Perhaps he had not even seen her. And when she returned to the corridor he was gone. He made no attempt to see her deliberately, nor did he telephone her again. It was over with. Done.

Jimmy was constantly underfoot at the apartment now. Once he tried to explain that Norman was terribly busy. He was working his head off on a new program. He had no time for girls or anything else but work.

Margie said quickly, "Lisa doesn't give a hoot what your friend Norman is doing. Let her alone."

"Let Lisa speak for herself," Jimmy said.

"Margie's right," Lisa told him. "Just because you're in the middle of a romance, don't get the idea that everybody else is too."

Jimmy stood by the radio exchanging grins with the Mexican pig. He felt in his pocket and found three pennies to drop through the slot in Pedro's side.

"You know," he said, "I liked that gold bow you dressed him up with for a while."

"Christmas is over," Lisa said shortly. Not even Margie knew that she had untied the bow and pulled the ribbon to shreds over a wastebasket. No more sentimental treasuring of a bit of ribbon for her.

Jimmy went on without turning around. "Norman's not the marrying kind, I guess. Not that he doesn't like girls. But I don't think he wants to settle for one girl at this stage of the game."

Margie had gone out to the kitchen and wasn't there to hush him. Lisa looked out the window and said nothing.

"I've heard him talk a bit on the subject." Jimmy stroked Pedro's snout affectionately. "His mother rushed into marriage when she

250

was too young to know what she was doing, and she regretted it plenty. He's seen what's happening with his stepmother too. I've tried to tell him there are all kinds of marriages, all kinds of people. Matter of fact, he got sore at me and blew his top. Norm is gun shy. Maybe when he's old and gray he'll settle down, but not now. I hope Reland realizes that."

Lisa said, "I couldn't care less."

But if what Jimmy said was true, then Reland certainly didn't realize it. The hardest thing to take was Reland's new glow of happiness. She bubbled over about her coming New Year's Eve date, and the other girls, glad to see her gay, encouraged her to talk about it. No one, it appeared, had ever taken Norman's dates with Lisa seriously, if they even knew about them.

On New Year's Eve, for want of anything better to do, Lisa offered to baby-sit for Beth and Bob so they could celebrate by themselves. Besides, this would give her the right to say that she had gone out on New Year's Eve – in case anybody asked.

So that was the way she welcomed the new year in – listening to television, which couldn't be avoided, and preventing the young Starlings from becoming too noisy or killing each other before the first of January

251

dawned. When the whistles began to blow, Bunny flung open the living room window and the girls stood shivering before it while they listened to the uproar of taxi horns, boat whistles, tin pans banging, and all the rest. Bunny, Mimi, and Carol blew horns madly and screamed "Happy New Year!" at the top of their lungs. The television set, turned up full volume, showed scenes of festivity around town, while bands played and New York went crazy.

Should auld acquaintance be forgot. . . .

There was no getting away from the tune and the hurt it brought. Lisa went into the dark kitchen and turned on the water faucet, pretending to get a glass of water. If she let go for one second she knew she would cry. And she didn't dare disgrace herself before the Starlings. This was the worst moment of all to be alone.

"Lisa, Lisa, where are you?" Bunny screamed. "Happy New Year, Lisa!"

She sipped her glass of water and blinked the tears away. Then she went back to the living room and hugged all three girls at once. Afterwards, when the children had gone to bed, she waited up until Beth and Bob came home, happy and tired, obviously in love with each other.

Christmas and New Year's Day were the

only two days when the guide service stopped, so Lisa could sleep the next morning. But her pillow was damp when she woke and she knew she had wept more than once during the night.

In the middle of the morning the phone rang and Margie ran to answer it. After an exchange of "Happy-New-Year's," she put her hand over the receiver and turned to Lisa, mouthing words.

"It's for you. Norman."

For just a second her heart leaped. But she was afraid to go to the phone, lest her voice tremble, lest she give her feelings completely away on this blue first of January.

She shook her head at Margie. "I can't talk to him. Tell him –" She was about to say, "Tell him I'm out," but Margie took matters into her own determined hands.

"She doesn't want to talk to you," she announced with gusto.

"Oh, no – you can't tell him that!" Lisa cried, but Margie had already hung up. She turned from the phone dusting her hands with an air of satisfaction.

"That will show him!"

There was no use scolding Margie about spilled milk. Nor could Lisa very well call Norman back. What had happened would be too hard to explain. It didn't matter anyway.

A New Year's Day call, however friendly, would not change Reland's prior claim, or Norman's interest in her. It was better not to talk to him until she could do it casually.

A gray and gloomy January gripped New York, with only occasional snow to brighten the scene. For a few hours city garbage cans wore round white berets which later turned to dirty water. Streets were briefly white, then muddy with slush, and taxi drivers grew short tempered.

A comparative quiet spread over the buildings of the United Nations. The General Assembly was no longer in session, the Security Council was not meeting, the crowds had thinned. And the job of being a guide, Lisa discovered, could be discouragingly dull and routine.

One morning she found herself standing before the plaster model of the UN buildings facing as blank a set of expressions as she had ever had turned toward her. She tapped the model with the pointer and went into her talk, wondering what good it did to pour herself out to ciphers like these. The group was obviously made up of idle sightseers doing the town. Probably they thought of coming here in the same breath as going to the top of the Empire State, or viewing Radio City. What the UN stood for would never get through to them. When she asked for questions there were none and she was not surprised. There was no spark anywhere in the blank stares turned upon her.

She marched them briskly off on the route, anxious to run through the job and be rid of them. They did all the things that could most annoy a guide. When she spoke of the terrazzo floor in the Secretariat lobby, the women clicked their heels against its hard surface, not listening to her at all. And they were more obviously impressed by the enormous area of carpeting in the buildings than by the work of the Trusteeship Council, where one of the men fell asleep. The women bounced in the seats of the visitors' galleries and the men fiddled with the earphones while Lisa droned on with her talk, not caring whether they listened or not.

Her own growing sense of antagonism fixed itself particularly on two of the faces that stared at her. Both were women, one past middle age, one fairly young. The older woman was dowdy and too fat for the dress size into which she had squeezed her reluctant flesh. Her mouth had a downward droop of disapproval and her eyes were dull. Certainly she was getting little out of Lisa's talk, and was resisting that little. Probably she had notions like Norman's father and shouldn't

255

have come on this tour in the first place.

The girl, on the other hand, merely looked stupid. She was blond, with a stolid, pale face and frowsy hair. Her eyes were a colorless hue and they stared unblinkingly without the slightest change of expression. Her stare was steady and seemed to have so little thought behind it that it irritated Lisa all the more. As far as questions went, the group was unusually dull. They shuffled and whispered among themselves or let their gaze wander toward anything but their guide.

This was, Lisa decided, the longest tour she had ever lived through, though when she got them down to the basement level and glanced at her watch, she found she was finishing ten minutes early. She thanked them automatically, pointed out further places of interest and said good-by in relief. They drifted away without comment, except for the woman with the unhappy mouth and the dull look in her eyes. She surprised Lisa by stepping up to her directly.

"I just want to tell you something, Miss," she said.

Lisa suppressed a sigh. All she wanted was to get away and rest her feet and not talk to people. But she had to be patient a moment longer.

"There is just one reason I came on this

tour," the woman went on. "I wanted an answer to something. I thought I might get it here today. My son died a few years ago in Korea. I wanted to know why. But I guess you couldn't tell me."

She turned and walked off, leaving Lisa staring after her in shocked silence. A soft voice spoke beside her and Lisa turned, startled, to see that the stolid blond girl had overheard. Her eyes were as pale, her face as expressionless, but there was surprising emotion in her voice.

"I heard," she said gently. "Do not mind. There is no answer to satisfy the heart for one like that. But for me – I want to tell you how it is fine, what you are doing here. There was a time – I remember very well when you talked just now about UNICEF. I was one of those children to whom milk was given. I remember how it is wonderful to stand in line and watch the kind faces of those who serve us. I remember a cold day when the cup of milk is warm in my hands. I hold it for a long time before I drink it. Today I have come here to say thank you."

She smiled and turned away before Lisa could find words to answer her. Lisa stood where she was for a long moment. She felt sick with shock clear through. When one of

257

the other guides spoke to her, she did not hear. There was only one place to take the reaction she was feeling. She turned toward the stairs.

Outside the Meditation Room the curtained corridor prepared one for quiet with its signs. There was no one in the room itself. She sat down and stared at the spreading green plant on the ancient tree trunk.

Tranquility lay about her, but within her own mind emotions were seething. She had never before felt so deep a scorn for herself, so deep a shame. She had never before been so completely conscious of failure that was entirely her own fault. And what was worse, failure in the face of great need. Who was she to look at the marks life had made upon the face of any human being and judge so lightly, so superficially?

For a little while longer she sat in the enfolding silence, asking now for help from something bigger than her own small self. She knew that she would long remember in her dreams the dull eyes and unhappy mouth of that woman in whose hands she might have placed some meaning that would comfort. Nor would she ever forget the irony of being reassured and thanked by the blond girl – when she herself deserved neither reassurance nor thanks.

When she left the quiet room and stepped into the lobby of the General Assembly building, she had lost any sense of self-importance. She could walk with her head up, but with humility in her heart. A sense of the importance of this uniting of nations had reached her more strongly than ever before. But any big thing was only as strong as its parts. Aggression had been stopped in Korea through the leadership of the United Nations, but it was the men who fought there – those who died and those who lived – who had done the stopping. And because of them the East was still free.

She phoned the dispatch desk and asked if she could be sent out on a tour again as soon as possible. The girl at the desk sounded surprised – this was an unusual request. But she must have sensed the urgency in Lisa's voice because after a moment's hesitation, she said, "Come along then. We can use you right away."

Lisa went back to the tour section knowing what she had to do. There was warm interest in the look she turned on those who waited for her, and it was strange how bright the faces of this group seemed in contrast to the last. There was one girl, with untidy, blond hair stuffed beneath an unbecoming hat, whose attentive gaze seemed vaguely familiar. Lisa smiled at her, and the girl smiled back, looking pleased. It was surprising, too, to see how eager this group was and how good were their questions. But now of course she knew why.

I am the tour, she thought wonderingly. I am what makes it, or breaks it. If the faces are dull, then they're only a reflection of my own.

When she was through and receiving the warm thanks of those who had followed her with so much interest, she knew she had done one of the best jobs ever. The girl with the untidy blond hair stepped up to her, chewing gum rapidly.

"So you made it?" she said. "You got to be a guide."

Lisa remembered her then – that girl on the very first tour she had taken. She held out her hand warmly.

"Why, it's you I have to thank for being here. If you hadn't opened my eyes. . . . How are you?"

The girl shook hands readily. "I don't get over here much any more. I got my weight down and now I got a uniform job myself. I'm an usher over in a Broadway movie house. But say – you sure do a swell job as a guide. And believe me, I know!"

Lisa felt that a special citation had been

given her. But even as she thanked the girl and turned away, she knew nothing could ever erase or make up for her earlier failure.

When she started toward the guides' lounge to check in by phone, she noticed Norman crossing the lobby. His eyes seemed to light as he saw her, and she couldn't help the way her foolish heart quickened. But he only smiled and spoke in passing and she knew it was better that way. She didn't want to be hurt any more.

18. V.I.P. Tour

During February troublesome matters began to stir in the Far East and the UN buzzed with rumors. It was likely that the Security Council would meet to discuss the problem. There was even talk of an emergency session of the General Assembly. News services and leading papers had offices in the Secretariat, and the news people were all on the alert.

Every evening Lisa listened to her father on the radio as he talked about the rising storm and the difficulties involved. The threat of war had long hung over the East and now it looked as if it might break into the

261

open at any minute. Lisa's mother wrote from Washington that Reid might come to New York in the event that the Security Council met.

If he came, Lisa thought, she would see to it that Norman Bond had a chance to meet him. Otherwise she tried to put all personal thoughts of Norman from her mind. Soon she must start looking for that future job and her plans and attention must be bent in that direction. She had no time to think of anything else. So she told herself. And always the thought of him ran like a deep current below the surface of her mind, and there was no way to channel it elsewhere.

Late in February news came through that the Security Council was to meet the following week and take up the Far Eastern question. When the day came, the General Assembly lobby sent up its muted roar to the cantilevered balconies. Lisa, showing a group how the lobby looked from above, could hear the sound that meant hundreds of people pouring in.

The tour guides were kept busy. During brief intervals in the lounge several girls asked Lisa whether her father was coming up for this session. But she didn't know for sure as yet. It would be like him to come suddenly, without warning.

Later that day, eating alone at a table in the cafeteria, she saw Norman come through the door and stand for a moment looking around the room. She could have told him that Reland's lunch hour was later today, but she felt too limp to make the effort. She looked out the window at the bleak gray river instead, to avoid meeting his eye.

When he crossed the room and stood beside her table, she had so schooled herself that on the surface she felt only surprise.

"You're the girl I'm looking for," he said. "Do you mind if I get a cup of coffee and sit down for a moment, Lisa? Reland's in a bit of a jam and maybe you could help her out."

She looked at him in astonishment. How could he ask *her* to help with Reland? How could he be so dense? But he seemed to take her agreement for granted and went after his coffee. The interval gave her time to strengthen her air of indifference against whatever might come up.

He was back in a moment to seat himself opposite her. "This is all pretty exciting, isn't it? I mean the Security meeting and all the possibilities that are in the air. Rumor has it your father may be coming to town."

"I hope he will come," Lisa said quietly.

"If he does, I'd like you to meet him."

"There's nothing I want more," he said. "Thanks for remembering."

There were a good many things she remembered. He was silent for a few moments looking off into space, and she wondered what he was thinking about. When he looked at her again he seemed uncomfortable, even a little embarrassed.

"I know you must think I have a lot of nerve," he said. "Breaking in on you like this when you told Margie you didn't want to talk to me, but –"

"What is it you want to tell me about Reland?" she asked directly. She didn't want him to tread on dangerous ground.

It seemed that he winced at her curt words, but he dropped the subject of the personal at once and spoke casually.

"You know she lives here with a private family? But now an aunt from California is coming to town on an unexpected visit to this family. Auntie takes it for granted that they will put her up and she's on her way. So Reland has to move out for a week until Auntie goes home. At least she feels she must help out by vacating her room."

Lisa said nothing. In New York there were plenty of places for Reland to go. She did not see where she came into the picture.

264

"The trouble is," said Norman, "that hotels are pretty expensive and Reland isn't getting any money from home. So I wondered if you and Margie could possibly put her up for just this coming week. Starting day after tomorrow. I know you don't have a spare room, but you have that day bed in the living room and Reland would be happy to make do with anything at all."

"Does Reland know you're arranging this?" Lisa asked.

"Oh, she didn't want me to bother you. But you've been kind to her before and perhaps this wouldn't be too much to ask. Of course if you feel it would inconvenience you –"

"I'd have to ask Margie," Lisa said.

"Margie has a heart as big as the harbor," Norman said confidently. "I'm sure it will be all right with her. Of course you have to ask her, but it's you I'm thinking about more than Margie."

What did he mean to imply? That she did not have a heart as big as Margie's?

He was looking at her in a rather strange way, smiling, and yet with something rather anxious behind the smile.

"Reland's had a rocky time," he said. "She knows you and Margie – it would be easier for her there."

He was right, Lisa knew. Her resistance

was due to her desire to stave off more hurt for herself. And that wasn't a good enough reason to refuse.

"If it's all right with Margie, it's all right with me," she told him. "I'll let you know if you'll phone me after eight o'clock tonight."

"That's wonderful," he said. "I knew you'd manage it." He drank the rest of his coffee in a gulp and stood up. "They've got us on the run downstairs today. I'll have to dash. Thanks a lot, Lisa. And don't forget about your father."

She looked after him feeling completely baffled. Why couldn't he have gone to one of the other guides who lived in an apartment? Men, she had to admit, were sometimes unfathomable.

That evening, while Margie was patting perfume behind her ears before going off to meet Jimmy, Lisa told her about Reland.

Margie set the perfume bottle down with a thump and stared at Lisa in the mirror. Disapproval was written all over her and Lisa felt too tired to argue. If Margie said, "No," then no it would be and she would tell Norman so.

Slowly Margie turned away from the dressing table. "I think it would be a wonderful idea," she said. Then she laughed out loud. "You do looked surprised. And I'll agree that I was ready to turn the whole thing

266

down at the first look. But maybe Norman's got something here. Maybe he's not as dumb as you think. Tell him we'd love to have her."

This was all beyond Lisa. Margie's kind of elaborate intrigue was not for her, and she didn't think it was for Norman either. Whatever Norman's motives, they were simple and uncomplicated. It was just that she didn't have the key that would enable her to read them.

When Norman phoned, she told him pleasantly that it would be all right for Reland to come. Margie had agreed. They would expect her.

"That's fine," Norman said in evident relief. "So will you invite her tomorrow, Lisa? She's so afraid of disturbing anyone that it will have to come from you direct."

This was just one more thing. It didn't matter.

"I'll ask her," Lisa said.

But when she proffered the invitation the following morning Reland looked doubtful. "I know Norman said he'd speak to you, but he really shouldn't have. I'll be crowding you too much and –" Reland broke off unhappily, plainly embarrassed.

"Please come," Lisa said, and tried to put sincerity into her voice. In none of this was

Reland to blame. "We'd both like to have you."

So it was agreed and Reland was grateful and happy again. But would this mean, Lisa wondered, that Norman would be over several times during Reland's stay? She would have to find something to do evenings that would take her out of the way.

To her surprise, on the day she brought Reland home, straight from work, she found that Margie had moved herself into the living room, and that Reland was to take over her place in the bedroom.

"You two girl guides will have a lot to talk about," Margie said, flicking her pony tail for emphasis. "Count me out of all that international stuff. It puts me to sleep."

But there was very little talk, international or otherwise, the first night Reland spent at the apartment. She seemed more hesitant and shy than ever. After a few efforts to start some sort of friendly conversation, Lisa left her alone and they went to bed in silence. Margie popped her head into the room to say good-night and remarked that they were certainly a pair of chatterboxes. But neither girl answered her.

Now the Security Council was meeting every day and the United Nations buildings were aboil with activity. One was likely to run into world figures in the diplomatic field in any elevator, any corridor. And of course, as a result of the meetings, outsiders trooped into the buildings and the tour guides worked steadily.

Asha, in particular, was happy these days. Several friends from India were in town in connection with the meetings, and she seemed to glow with a quiet pleasure over these contacts with her homeland.

Reland, watching her one day in the lounge, nodded her understanding. "Nothing makes a fellow a bigger patriot than to be away from home for a while. It's not the big things that make you homesick so much as it is the little ones. Sometimes I think life would settle down completely if I could have a good British tea every afternoon, with thin bread and butter and little cakes. Tea that had never been disguised by a tea bag."

One of the American girls who had traveled abroad laughed. "That's the beginning of the end, Reland. You'll be going home any day now. I can remember how open-mindedly I went to England a couple of years ago. I wasn't going to be an American abroad. I was going to accept all the customs of the country exactly as they were. So after my first shock of horror, I ate stone-cold toast morning after morning for breakfast. But in two months I began to yearn for a piece of American toast, so hot from the toaster it would burn my fingers. And I knew it was time for me to come happily home."

Some of the other foreign girls began to talk about their own small likes and dislikes, and always there was an undercurrent of yearning for home, though the word meant a different place to each one.

Listening, Lisa thought about this facet of the picture. Men needed a uniting of nations, it was true, but they needed this other thing too – a love of the mountains and rivers and soil of one land. She could remember the way she felt as a little girl when she sang the words, "for amber waves of grain..." and felt all the richness of American land stretching to every side of her.

A small voice spoke softly in the room. "How sad the exile who cannot return to his own country."

That was Jeanie Soong, and the ripple of a sigh went through the room. There were others who were exiles too.

Late that afternoon when Lisa had finished what she hoped was her last tour for the day, she got back to the lounge to find a message waiting for her. She was to call dispatch at once.

270

"Hello," said the girl at the desk when Lisa had dialed the number. "Sorry not to let you go now, but there's a V.I.P. here we want to send on a special tour to the Secretary-General's office. Will you take him up?"

Would she! She'd take anybody and anything to get up to that office. Some of the guides had wangled a visit in one way or another, though mostly during the summer months when the office stood empty. Otherwise there was no excuse for a UN guide, whose headquarters was in the basement, to get up to the 38th floor.

"Look me over," Lisa said to the girls in the lounge as she checked grooming details before the mirror. "I'm taking a V.I.P. up to the Secretary-General's office."

There were wails from girls who hadn't been chosen, but they wished her luck, and Judith said, "Chip us off a piece of his desk for a souvenir." Lisa went upstairs laughing and hurried to dispatch.

The girl at the desk wore an odd look, as though she were trying hard to be solemn. "See that you make a good impression," she whispered. "This is a responsibility we're handing you."

"Who is it?" Lisa said softly. "Do I know him?"

"Could be," said the girl. "He's right

271

behind you against the far wall. Good luck."

Lisa turned and looked across the room. There was a big, dark-haired man sitting alone at one end of the bench. He had taken some papers from a briefcase and was working on them with a pencil. Lisa suppressed a youthful whoop of joy and flung herself across the room.

Reid Somers saw her coming and rose to greet her with a bear hug, much to the interest of those who waited to go on tour.

"Dad!" she cried. "When did you get here? Is Mother here too?"

He rubbed a cheek that was faintly bristly against hers, just as he used to when she was little. "She came up with me, but she can only stay a day. Ted has something cooking at school and she wants to be there. I left her at the hotel, but since I'm tied up for a while tonight she's going to head over to your place to see Beth and Bob and then find out if she can take you to dinner."

"Of course she can!" Lisa said happily.

Somehow she felt better than she had in weeks. Maybe she wasn't quite so self-sufficient as she'd thought. Everybody needed someone of her own. And she had no one here in New York.

"Am I really to take you up to the Secretary-General's office?"

272

"You are indeed. And we'd better get started. You wrote in one of your letters that the one thing in the building you still wanted to see was that office. So I thought perhaps we could manage it together. I have an informal date to see him before my broadcast tonight. You know we were friends a long while ago in Europe. Besides, with my book, I have an official reason too."

Lisa became aware of the interest centered upon her father and slipped back into the correct behavior of a guide. "I'll show you the way," she said and walked with him through the corridor that led to the Secretariat building.

Going up in the elevator father and daughter looked at each other contentedly, slipping quickly back into an affectionate relationship. There was so much to talk about, so much to tell each other, but it could wait a little while until Mother was there too. The elevator sped upward with so little movement, so little sound, that only the faint pressure in the ears betrayed its rise.

"I've never set foot on this floor," Lisa whispered as they left the car and walked toward a desk where a guard was on duty. Lisa told him their business and he motioned them to a pleasant lounge behind the desk and lifted the receiver of a phone.

They did not sit down, however. The great glass windows that walled the sides of the Secretariat building drew them, and they went to look out toward the east, far above the river. Here they were on the edge of Manhattan, with their backs to the city itself.

As they stood for a few moments, waiting and admiring the view, Lisa found herself wondering if Norman had ever been up here. She wished she could tell him about this visit. He would appreciate how she felt about coming here. Thinking of Norman reminded her.

"Dad," she said, "do you remember the announcer from the UN radio department who was on the program when I appeared? He wants very much to meet you. He's more than just a fan because he'd like to do your sort of thing some day."

Her father always had a lively interest in people, and a special sympathy toward youth. He never grew impatient about his fans as the rest of the family sometimes did.

"Of course I'd like to meet him," he said. "Since your mother and I are planning to take you to lunch tomorrow in the delegates' dining room, why not invite him to come along?"

"Oh – lunch isn't necessary," Lisa said

quickly. "He just wants to –"

"Best time for me," her father said. "Bring him along." He turned from the window. "Here you are, Miss Tour Guide, it looks as though someone is coming for us."

An attractive young woman came down the corridor to speak to the guard. She approached them and introduced herself as Miss Hill.

"The Secretary-General is out just now," she told Reid Somers. "But he is expecting you. Won't you come in and wait for him?" She smiled a thank-you at Lisa and turned to lead the way toward the office.

"This is my daughter," Mr. Somers said quickly. "I wonder – if he's out just now, do you suppose she could have a glimpse of his offices?"

Miss Hill smiled. "Of course. We're so used to thinking that you guides know the whole building that we forget you don't get up here very often."

There was a second lounge, with offices opening off the sides, and beyond it the room that was the heart of this entire building. Lisa stepped into it, aware at once of the quiet, the hush that lay upon the room. Battles of words might be fought downstairs and tempers might rise, but here was a place of peace in the center of the whirlwind.

Her eyes were drawn at once to the west wall. It was painted a light gray and was bare of any decoration except for a nearly life-size head and torso of an East Indian goddess carved in dark-gray weathered stone. The figure wore a high headdress and her long-fingered hands were bent in the manner of the Eastern dance.

Miss Hill noted their interest. "The Goddess of Thunder and Lightning," she said. "She came from an Indian temple as a gift to the Secretary-General."

The figure was striking against the stark, bare wall. Glancing about, Lisa saw that the rest of the room was both severe in its Scandinavian simplicity and beautiful because of it. Pale-hued pine cabinets lined the entire end of the room behind the Secretary-General's desk, and of course the east side was one great window, with wide Venetian blinds which could shut out the glare of the morning sun. On the wall near the door was a modern painting and Miss Hill explained that the Museum of Modern Art loaned all the paintings used in these rooms and changed them every few months.

In one corner there were comfortable chairs and a low table with ash trays upon it. Opposite the great desk was a long table with magazines and papers laid out across it.

Except for a small open bookcase there were no other furnishings. On the window ledge at the left of the desk sat a small "squawk box," such as all offices in the Secretariat had ready for use. Lisa knew you could push its buttons and bring in any program being broadcast from the UN.

Miss Hill said, "Come along and I'll show you the rest."

She led them through a long conference room decorated with the flags of the Member nations and then to a lounge and private dining room on the other side of the building. There was a kitchen adjoining this where meals could be cooked, so the Secretary-General could have a few people to luncheon when he chose.

But Lisa hardly heard what Miss Hill was saying because of the dramatic sight that spread suddenly before them. She caught her breath and stepped close to her father, sharing this moment of wonder with him.

Here the glass windows faced west and at five o'clock dusk was seeping through the canyons of New York. Lights had come on in the great buildings that marched the length of Manhattan. There they stood – the titans: the Chrysler Building, Radio City, the Empire State and all the others – one long gray line glittering with golden lights. Behind glowed a red sky where the sun had just set, fading upward into rose and saffron. It was so beautiful that Lisa felt tears sting her eyes.

"Two extremes coming together," her father said softly. "Beauty made by God and beauty made by man."

The glow began to fade even as they stood breathless, watching. In a little while only the vast area of buildings, lit by millions of lights, stood out against the graying sky.

Reid Somers turned to Miss Hill. "Thank you," he said simply.

She nodded in understanding. "We have people here from everywhere. Men who've seen the Taj Mahal and the pyramids and all the wonderful sights of the world. But every one of them is speechless when he sees this."

They moved about. Lisa saw the fireplace on one side of the room – a skyscraper fireplace that really worked! Miss Hill invited Mr. Somers to sit down to wait for the Secretary-General and Lisa said she'd have to run along. Especially since Mother would be waiting for her.

"I'll join you after my broadcast," her father said. "I'm doing it from the studio here, so I haven't far to go."

Lisa was quiet all the way downstairs. She didn't want to break the spell.

19. World Affairs and Woman Affairs

It was good to see her mother again. Lisa found her visiting happily with Reland and Margie. They went out to dinner and came home in time to catch part of Reid Somers's broadcast. Tonight even Margie listened attentively.

When he had finished his discussion of the latest turn in the world crisis, he told the radio audience that he had seen something he would never forget tonight, something he wished they all might share. Lisa closed her eyes as he described the view of steel and concrete sprinkled with light, silhouetted against the sunset sky. She could see the whole thing clearly again as he spoke.

When the broadcast was over, she slipped into the hall off the living room to phone Norman and see whether he could join them for lunch the next day. He had listened to the broadcast too and was delighted over the opportunity to meet her father.

Lisa couldn't help adding the one thing she had wanted to tell him. "I was up there with

Dad tonight in the Secretary-General's suite. I saw that sunset too. There aren't any words for it, Norman."

"I know," he said. "I felt it when he was describing it."

When she hung up and went back to join the others she felt more lighthearted than she had for a long while. There was something special to look forward to tomorrow.

Since the following day was Lisa's day off, she was not in uniform, but wore a blue-gray suit, with a strand of pearls at the neck, and a lapel pin and earrings of tiny white flowers – a gift from her mother after a trip to Paris.

"Very nice," her mother said in approval when they met in the UN lobby before going upstairs to the dining room, where Mr. Somers and Norman would look for them. "And you, Lisa? You seemed very happy at Christmas –"

Lisa spoke quickly. "Of course I'm happy. I love what I'm doing. Everything is fine."

But she was glad when they reached the escalator. Sometimes her mother saw too much.

The luncheon went off very well. They had a table overlooking the garden in the delegates' spacious dining room. Dad had a way of drawing people out, and Norman talked readily and without any awe of her father, for all his admiration for him. Dad liked him and Lisa felt a little proud of them both. Not that all the talk turned on serious matters. Her mother was always ready to put in a light word at the right moment. When there was laughter, her mother would look quickly at her husband, and there would be a moment when their eyes met and there was a sharing between them of the fun.

She had seen that all her life, Lisa thought, and always taken it for granted. But now she was sharply conscious of the feeling between them. Couldn't Norman look at Katherine and Reid Somers and see how different a good marriage relationship could be from what he had witnessed in his own home? Couldn't he see that it was possible?

Norman had begun to speak about his own father in response to something Mr. Somers had said. "I'm afraid Dad belongs to a school of thought that is, thank goodness, dying out. He feels that the United States is only safe behind its own walls and there is too great a risk in getting into the world's affairs."

Mr. Somers nodded. "It's surprising that there are still those who forget that no walls are high enough today. To live with honor means to take a risk. Yet in our eagerness to get away from this sort of thinking, the

United States has sometimes rushed in with too much forceful enthusiasm and tried to change things too rapidly in other countries. I believe the United Nations does a wise job of starting where people are."

"Sometimes though," Norman said, "the progress is so slow that it all seems hopeless."

"That's when we look ahead to all we want to accomplish. But when we look back —" Mr. Somers's eyes lighted — "we know how far we've come. What is it Trygve Lie says — that we must be prepared for the worst, while still struggling for the best?"

"But what hope is there for the best?" Norman asked. "What *is* the best?"

Lisa's mother answered quickly. "Peace with freedom. For people everywhere."

Her husband nodded. "I don't think men will ever stop struggling for that, no matter what the setbacks or defeats. This struggle isn't new; it's as old as history. And our chances for it now are better than they've ever been. But democracy is on trial right now with the world's underprivileged. The UN's program of technical assistance is raising our rating tremendously with those people. And there's the work UNESCO and UNICEF and all the rest are doing. I don't think we can afford to sit back and refuse to help because we don't like the prospect of the worst that can happen. Or because our efforts are often misunderstood. There's too much to be done."

Norman smiled wryly. "I suppose my dad believes in survival of the fittest, and he has a notion that *we* are the fittest. The old jungle law."

"Men can't live by jungle law," Lisa's mother said. "The strong must fight for the weak."

"More than that," said Mr. Somers. "The weak need to be helped to help themselves. That's where true strength lies. We need to remember that both within and without our own borders."

Norman nodded. "You put it very well, sir. And of course it's what I believe."

Lisa was watching him, pleased, when he looked at her. Their eyes met and held for just an instant and it seemed to Lisa that a current of understanding sprang between them. It was almost as if Norman had reached out to touch her hand. Then she dropped her gaze uneasily and the moment was gone. It could not have existed.

Both Mr. Somers and Norman were on work schedules, and the meal could not go on too long. So, all too soon, Lisa and her mother told them good-by and took a cab over to town.

A shopping spree was fun and Lisa hated to take her mother to the station afterwards and see the train roll in. Later, as she rode a cross-town bus back to the apartment, she thought about the talk at lunch and of how Norman and her father had warmed to each other. But she would not be seeing Norman again under such pleasant circumstances.

She remembered Reland back at the apartment, dreading the evening ahead.

Margie was not taking turns with the cooking these days. She was, she said, practicing. Nearly every meal was a new concoction, with Lisa acting as a guinea pig. She and Jimmy planned on a June marriage and Margie's recipe file had begun to bulge.

When Lisa reached home she found Reland on her knees in the middle of the living room floor, building card houses with Bunny and Mimi. Margie, as usual, was in the kitchen. Reland looked up in greeting as Lisa came in, but Mimi had her small nose on the carpet, her pink panties up in the air, and paid no attention to her arrival. Nor did Bunny, who lay stretched full length with her chin on the card house level. It seemed that something stupendous was about to happen.

"Poke him, Mimi!" Bunny screeched. "Make him walk so the roof will fall in."

Mimi poked obligingly. There was evidence

of a scrambling movement beneath the cards and they heaved in earthquake fashion. The card house collapsed, slithering cards in every direction, and a small brown turtle trundled slowly out of the wreckage. Mimi squealed in delight and Bunny picked up the turtle. Gathering up the cards, Reland smiled at Lisa.

"Mrs. Starling had to take Carol to the dentist, so we have company for a little while. I'm showing them a game I used to play back home in Scotland when I was little and my uncle brought me a turtle."

"Hello, girls," Lisa said, pulling off her hat. "It looks like fun. But won't your new turtle make the monster jealous?"

"Oh, he's taking a nap, silly old thing," said Bunny carelessly.

Mimi sat up and looked at Lisa with curious brown eyes. "What monster?" she asked.

"You all right?" Bunny reached out and put a hand on her sister's forehead. "You got a temperature or something?"

"Of course I'm all right." Mimi wriggled away from her hand. "All I said was, *what monster.*"

"*Your* monster, of course," Bunny told her.

Lisa added. "That's the one I meant. I hope there aren't any others."

"I don't know what you're talking about,"

Mimi said and reached out to take the turtle from Bunny's hand.

"You don't know –" Bunny began in outrage, not even trying to get the turtle back.

Lisa shook a silencing finger at her. "Wait, Bunny. Let's get to the bottom of this. Mimi, we're all under the impression that there has been a monster around here for quite a while, and that you were its chief owner. Isn't that right?"

"Oh, that one," said Mimi, poking at the turtle so that he pulled in his head and feet. "That was just a make-believe one I made up when I was little. There really isn't any monster."

Bunny looked as if she were about to explode, but Mimi paid no attention. She set the turtle on the palm of her hand and blew on it calmly. As far as she was concerned the last word had been spoken.

"I believe this will take a bit of adjusting for us all," Reland said, getting up from her knees. "I'll miss him quite a bit – that monster."

"I belong to the old order too," Lisa admitted. "Life isn't going to be the same around here."

She went into the bedroom to take off her things. Reland followed her to the door.

"Norman phoned that he'd like to come

over tonight. Do you mind, Lisa?"

"Of course not." Lisa turned her back, rummaging in a dresser drawer. "Margie probably has a date, and I'm going out tonight. So you can have the place to yourselves."

"Oh," said Reland softly, and went back to the living room without comment.

She hadn't intended to go out tonight, Lisa thought. She'd meant to stay home and catch up on chores. But she couldn't sit around and watch Norman and Reland together. There was nothing to do except get out of the way.

After dinner she escaped as quickly as she could, pleading an appointment for which she was late. She wished she had known about this sooner. Dad was tied up tonight, but she might have made a date with Jeanie or Asha for the evening. Now she would have to go to a neighborhood movie alone.

The theater was showing a double feature, with neither picture one she cared about. But she sat through both and even saw part of the first one over again. When it was late enough, she went back to the apartment.

A lamp burned in the living room, but Margie and Jimmy weren't home. Only a reflected glow from outside lighted the bedroom. Reland had gone to bed and Lisa undressed quietly in the dark so as not to waken her.

As she crept under the blanket, Reland's bed creaked and Lisa knew she was awake. She had a feeling that the other girl had turned on her side to watch her in the dim room. The silence was one of something about to start. Lisa yawned and rolled over, her back to the other bed. Whatever Reland might say, she didn't want to hear. But Reland's words, when they came, surprised her.

"We're both pretty much in love with Norman, aren't we?" Reland said softly.

Lisa stiffened under the blanket. This was not a subject she wanted to open with Reland, and it surprised her that the other girl had broached it. What except hurt could lie in discussion?

"At any rate, I am," Reland went on. "I know you're thinking about Phil, wondering how I could have changed. But I haven't changed. Not really. There's part of me that will always love Phil and never forget him. But Norman has said all along that I'd have to accept reality, instead of trying to run away from it. And now I think I am. So perhaps I'm falling in love with Norman. If only –"

She paused and the room was quiet, except for the distant roar of New York. Lisa did not speak. She felt as tense as if she were braced against a blow about to fall. But she had no contribution of her own to make.

"Do you mind very much if I think out loud a little?" Reland asked.

"Will it help any?" Lisa said.

"It might do a bit of good. Especially if you would talk too. So I could know what you're thinking and how you feel."

Lisa stirred uneasily. "There isn't anything I can say."

"That's not what Margie thinks. Margie says you've fallen hard for Norman. Those are the very words she used. And she also said she thought I was just trying to fill the emptiness by making myself believe I was in love again."

"Margie has no business getting into this," Lisa said.

"I don't think that would stop Margie." There was faint laughter in Reland's tone – laughter that might be close to tears. "She gave me something to think about. I believe she's partly right. But there's more to it than that. No matter how it began, or why I reached out to Norman, it's turning real for me. That's why I have to stop it. And you ought to stop it too, Lisa."

"What do you mean?" Lisa was startled. If Reland stepped out of the picture, then the thing that tugged at her conscience, made her feel vaguely guilty, would be removed.

"Because Norman isn't for either of us," Reland said sadly. "He's too much afraid of marriage. He has set up an impossible ideal of the only woman he will marry. He hasn't said all this, but I've sensed it. Perhaps because I've known him longer than you have. He wants what he believes would be a perfect marriage – without friction, without clashes or quarrels, without tears or division. I'm sure he likes us both, but we both frighten him a little. He doesn't want to get seriously involved."

"I should think you'd be just right for him," Lisa said in a small voice. "You're much more gentle than I am. You'd try your best to please him and I think there wouldn't be the antagonism that sometimes crops up between Norman and me."

"I know," Reland agreed calmly. "But he hates tears, he hates emotional women. I get emotional and worry him. While you are so bent on *being* somebody in your own right that you worry him too. I don't think he wants a career girl for a wife. If you could change that – but I don't suppose you can, any more than I can remember not to be emotional."

"I don't want to change," Lisa said. "I

want to be me. I want a man who will value the things I am – not one who'll try to change me into something else."

"I know," Reland said. "That would be a very comfortable way for either of us to have it. But perhaps never to change is never to grow."

For a little while there was silence, broken at length by Reland's whisper, almost as if she spoke to herself alone.

"There is one thing it's good to know. When a person has been hurt terribly and deeply, nothing else can ever again hurt quite so much. One dies a little, perhaps, but goes on living. I know now that it's possible to do that, and so I am stronger than I was before. I shall never be so vulnerable again."

Lisa lay still, touched by her words. She knew that Reland had gently tendered her a gift. She had said in effect: "If it is you he loves, don't worry about me." Now Lisa wanted very much to be as generous as Reland. She reached across the gap between the two beds and lightly touched the other girl's hand. For an instant Reland's fingers closed gratefully about hers.

Then they heard the front door open and Margie come in. After that both pretended to be asleep. Under the tea cosy – about which Reland had laughed – the hum of the clock was scarcely louder than her soft breathing. Lisa listened for a long while before she fell asleep.

In the morning Reland said cheerfully from the other bed, "Very soon now I think I shall go home to Scotland."

20.   *The Highest Dream*

Reland stayed with them for the rest of the week, and twice Norman came to see her. One time Lisa managed to be out with her father and the second time she went again to a movie. So she did not have to face him at all. Reland was sweet and quiet and helpful around the apartment, and she did not again bring up the dangerous topic of Norman.

Once Margie asked Lisa if she'd had any "girl talk" with Reland. When Lisa turned the question aside Margie regarded her wisely.

"I thought it might do you two some good to get together," she said. "Clear the air with a good blow. Then one of you could go to work on Norman."

"Please stay out of this, Margie," Lisa told her. "Norman isn't the sort of man who can be managed like Jimmy."

"Oh?" said Margie. "A new species?"

Lisa regarded her roommate helplessly. "I don't want a man I can boss. He's got to make up his own mind."

Margie said, "Pussyfeathers!" unsympathetically and Lisa walked out of the room.

Perhaps there was truth of some sort in all these things people were saying to her. But she wasn't like Margie, or like Reland. If there was an answer it didn't seem to lie in someone else's approach.

Both the European and Asiatic girls at the UN sometimes spoke with a tinge of scorn about American women as wives. American women were spoiled, they said. American men no longer knew how to be men. Lisa had listened uncomfortably to more than one such discussion. An American marriage – a good one – was more of a partnership, she felt, with the woman helping to earn and develop herself as an individual, not just as a shadow born to serve her husband. And a good part of the time she managed to be a good mother and keep a bright, clean home at the same time. If she was sometimes too tired to run for her husband's pipe and slippers in the traditional fashion at night, she was alert enough mentally to talk to him at the dinner table and be an interesting person in her own right. It had seemed to Lisa sometimes that

293

even as they criticized, the girls from abroad looked with a certain envy at the freedom and independence of the American woman.

At the UN the Security Council meetings and the talk went on and on. But now there was a mounting tension as events moved toward a crucial vote.

During the following week, after Reland had left, Lisa had an unexpected phone call from Mrs. Schermer in the publicity office of UNICEF, reminding her that she had promised to come ur for a talk one of these days. Would it be possible this afternoon? Lisa arranged her time and went upstairs as soon as she could.

Mrs. Schermer awaited her in a pleasant, bright office, high in the Secretariat building, her desk beside windows overlooking the East River. Lisa took the chair opposite, glancing at a circular stand displaying UNICEF pamphlets and materials.

Mrs. Schermer removed her dark-rimmed glasses and smiled at Lisa purposefully.

"I'll come right to the point," she said. "Have you made any plans as to what you will do when you leave the guide service?"

Lisa shook her head. "I'm afraid I haven't. I suppose I haven't really looked as yet."

"Perhaps you won't need to. What would

you think of coming to work for us?"

Lisa was startled. "I can't imagine any department I'd rather work for, but – what would I do?"

"Public relations of a special type. The woman who handled this is leaving in the summer, and there seems to be no one else in the department quite fitted to do the sort of thing we want. I've had an eye on you ever since those two broadcasts, Miss Somers. And we've sent several school talks your way to see how you would handle them. That's what we want – a *young* person, whom other young people will readily like and who can give spirited, moving talks. Other guides do well, but you have a particular quality – and you are also good on radio and television."

Lisa made an involuntary gesture. "Talking to young people would be fine, but radio and television aren't for me."

"Why not?" Mrs. Schermer asked bluntly.

"My father," Lisa said. "I can't be another Reid Somers, and I don't want to spend my life apologizing because I'm not as good as he is."

"That is completely foolish," said Mrs. Schermer without mercy. Yet there was a kindness in her eyes that softened the words. "You would be doing entirely different work. On the radio you have a personality which

295

is distinctly your own. Not everyone can come through on voice alone. You do. Of course the salary we could pay would not be overwhelming. Everyone in the department starts at the same rate of pay."

"Please don't think I'm ungrateful," Lisa told her. "And money isn't the main consideration. But I don't know. As I say – my father –"

"We're not considering you as Reid Somers's daughter," Mrs. Schermer said. "We would be buying you for what you can do. Call yourself Sally Smith, if you like."

This was the most convincing thing Mrs. Schermer had said. But before Lisa could answer, a girl came to the door of the office and signaled with a forefinger. Mrs. Schermer thanked her with a nod and turned a switch on the "squawk box" on her desk. Dave Morgan's voice came over the loudspeaker, speaking in French. He often did his coverage of UN affairs in both English and French.

Lisa knew what this meant even before he got to the translation. The vote had been taken in the Security Council. As a top reporter Dave allowed no emotion to color his words, but Lisa sensed what he must be feeling. The veto had been cast. Mrs. Schermer flipped the switch despairingly and stared at Lisa.

"There!" she cried. "That is why you must

come and work for us – to help counteract that!"

"What – do you mean?" Lisa faltered.

Mrs. Schermer drummed the surface of her desk with nervous fingers. "Don't you see what this means? I'm not referring to the blocking of action in the Security Council, but to the stories that will break in the evening and morning papers, and go out on every broadcast tonight: *The United Nations fails again!* As if all the work we are doing here hinged on that one thing that gets so much publicity. Oh, it make me furious!"

Lisa waited, abashed, silent.

"I know the way the papers will play this up," Mrs. Schermer went on, "and how people will react. Yet right now in the Far East a wholesale stamping out of ferocious diseases that have killed millions of people is going on. Even the poorest governments are working with the UN and paying what they can, so that people are helping themselves. There's flood control in Greece; in Haiti a new way of breeding fish for food, taught that country by Indonesia. And there are new tools for the farmer in Afghanistan – all because people are exchanging their skills through the United Nations, helping one another to live better lives. Yet the headlines will scream about the veto, and the uninformed will say the UN doesn't work. How can we wake people up? How can we make them understand?"

She halted her vehement words and stared out the great window beside her, paying no attention now to Lisa. After a few moments she turned back and said:

"Well?"

Lisa edged forward in her chair. "I have very little confidence in my ability," she said humbly, "but if you can use me, I'd like to try."

The older woman smiled warmly, but her acceptance was calm, as if she had never doubted the outcome. "When can you come to us?"

"I must finish my year as a guide," Lisa said. "But I need not stay for the second year. September perhaps?"

Mrs. Schermer stood up and held out her hand and Lisa rose to take it. "Thank you, my dear. September it shall be. In the meantime there will be more school talks. The guide service is cooperative about those, allowing you girls to speak on your working time."

Going downstairs in the elevator, Lisa felt tingly with elation. The cloud of uncertainty that had hung over her for so long was gone. She had a direction now, and even if some of the ramifications frightened her a little, it was a wonderful feeling. She wished her father were still in town so she could run to him with the news. But he had returned to Washington days ago. And now, more than anyone else, she wanted to tell Norman. It was foolish to hesitate, to avoid him. He liked her and he would be glad. It was as simple as that.

She waited until after dinner. Margie was home tonight, so she went downstairs to the pay booth in the lobby where she wouldn't be overheard, and dialed his number. He answered and she told him of her interview with Mrs. Schermer. He was as pleased as she knew he would be.

"It's terrific," he said. "Reid Somers can look to his laurels with competition like this."

"I'm not that good, and I'm not competing with Dad," Lisa said quickly. "But I've found out something about me this afternoon. All along I've been thinking the main thing was to *be* somebody. To make a big name for myself – as if that was the only way I could live up to Dad. But, Norman, I don't believe that's really the answer. I've just discovered that I want to *do* something more than I want to be somebody."

There was a little pause at the other end of the line and then Norman said, "I like you, Lisa Somers. I like you very much. And do

299

you know – you *are* somebody."

It was her turn to be at a loss for words, but before she could speak again, he shifted from the personal.

"It looks as though an emergency session of the General Assembly may be called. Our department's full of rumors. A vote by any seven members of the Security Council can do it, you know."

"Or a two-thirds majority vote among the members of the General Assembly," Lisa added, playing guide automatically. "How long would it take to call a meeting?" This was something she didn't know.

"Could be done in a day or so, I expect. Though I don't suppose they'll act that fast. Anyway, it looks as though we're in for a bit of excitement before the end of the week."

They talked about the UN problems that played so large a part in their daily lives and then Norman thanked her for calling him and they hung up.

For just a moment Lisa sat in the dim privacy of the booth, wondering where to go next. But there was no use in mooning here. She must hurry upstairs and write a letter to Mother and Dad about her promised job.

The rest of the week she saw nothing of Norman. On an international scale matters were moving toward a climax.

A request had been made by a Member nation for the calling of an emergency session of the General Assembly. During the week Member nations were polled, the simple majority vote achieved. And on Saturday the Assembly would meet.

A sense of activity and mounting excitement swept through the three buildings. It was as though a great heart had begun to throb, and all the life of the place tuned itself to the rhythm of the one beat.

The guides were briefed every day on new developments, armed with the answers to a great many questions sure to come up during their tours. Facilities that sometimes grew slack in the off-season months, sprang to oiled working order. Disconnected phones in the delegates' lounges now responded to the dial, and towels no longer ran out in the washrooms. Special reporters from the nation's press descended upon the building to reinforce a staff already in operation. The heart was beating and the muscles and nerves and arteries waited for the brain to command.

Lisa almost regretted the fact that she had been promoted to Saturdays off and wouldn't be on duty during the following day when the G.A. was scheduled to open its meeting.

On Friday evening Norman waited for her after work.

"You're going to have a look at the meeting tomorrow, aren't you?" he began without preliminary. "This is something you'll want to use in your school talks – give 'em a real picture of the Assembly in action."

"I do want to," Lisa said. "I'm planning to come over during the day."

"Make it right after lunch," Norman said, "and come down to the radio department. I'm not going to be the most valuable member of the staff tomorrow and maybe I can take you upstairs if there's an empty booth. Give you a look at the show from a different angle than the way you see it from the rear in the visitors' gallery."

"I'd love that!" Lisa cried. "Thanks for thinking of me."

He hesitated. "I think of you quite a lot," he said almost doubtfully. "Well – we're set then. I'll see you tomorrow."

He didn't offer to walk her home and she went by herself thoughtfully. Somehow, as she was just beginning to realize, the talk with Reland had cleared the air. *Be natural,* she told herself. *Be yourself and take it easy. That's all you need to do. Don't rush after him, but don't withdraw yourself either.* This was a little like the truth Mimi had suddenly grown up to. There weren't any monsters except the ones you made up yourself.

Reland too had given her a truth. She had said that never to change was never to grow. Lisa knew now quite humbly that she wanted both to change and to grow. It had been foolish not to realize that she too must adapt to others. To be oneself was not to be unyieldingly so.

That evening, paging through handwritten sheets she had copied at various times into a notebook, all concerned with the UN, she read again two lines of a poem by Thomas Curtis Clark.

"Let us no more be true to boasted race or clan,
But to our highest dream, the brotherhood of man."

How much more these words meant to her now, after months of working in the United Nations. No man could help, or should help, loving his family, his school, his town, his country, but in so doing he must never forget the still higher dream in which all peace was rooted. A bit of this dream was hers, too. It was a grave and personal responsibility.

She waited eagerly for time to pass so she could go over for the glimpse Norman had promised her. In the morning she listened to introductory speeches on the radio. Some speakers were interesting, some dull, merely mouthing platitudes. But all were the voices of nations – big and little – making themselves heard on an international scale, as they had never been heard before in the history of the world.

After the noon hour adjournment she had lunch and then hurried over, crossing through traffic opposite the semi-circle of flags. How bright the day was with spring, and how heartening these flags, their rainbow colors lifting in the breeze, the brass knobs on every pole brilliant in the midday light. She had sensed the dream the first time she had seen them.

Sunlight flooded the plaza as she crossed it and set the river sparkling. Today she was out of uniform as she joined the crowds filing through revolving doors. She took the nearest stairway down and went easily through the maze that had once confused her. Norman looked out the door of the radio department just as she came up.

"Good timing, Lisa. Come along. I spotted an empty booth this morning and if it's still clear we can watch there for a while."

They went upstairs, past guards who recognized them and let them by, and through a door almost concealed at the end of a curved blue wall. Here narrow stairs led up and down to the two levels of booths, and the passageway was tight as those backstage in a theater. Norman led her past a row of doors, stopping at one to which he had a key. She had never been here before, so it was all new and interesting.

The booth was small, but not cramped in space. Its chief feature was the plate glass window that covered one side and slanted outward into the auditorium beyond. She saw at once that she could lean into the window and look down and to both sides as if in the room. A black ledge that formed a desk rimmed the window inside. There was an amplifier overhead, now turned off, and a telephone.

"Doesn't it interrupt a speech if a phone rings while you're here?" Lisa asked.

"They've thought of that." Norman pointed out tiny bulbs on the ledge that would light when a call was put through.

Lisa rested her hands on the ledge and leaned into the window. The great room below was already filling with people. The visitors' galleries were packed at both levels, while delegates milled about in the floor aisles, or stood or sat at their places behind long, green-covered tables, talking to one another. The pink marble desk on the dais was empty, waiting. The glass of the opposing radio and news booths reflected the bright blue and beige of the delegates' leather chairs. In the booth next to theirs the window had been opened and a camera set up ready to photograph the scene.

As she watched, Lisa saw the Secretary-General come in, with the Executive Secretary beside him. He greeted the Assembly president and spoke to others on the floor. Then the three men went up to the platform together and took their places at the great desk. On a level just below them was the speaker's rostrum, looking a little like an organ, with a lowered well for notes and a light above it. This desk could be raised or lowered to suit the height and convenience of the individual speaker, and had sometimes surprised the uninitiated when it was manipulated without warning from a distance.

Now the delegates were taking their seats and Norman turned on the amplifier. At once the sound of the room came into the quiet booth, the all-pervading hum of voices. In a moment the president of the Assembly brought down his gavel and the afternoon meeting was in session.

Lisa sat in the small chair Norman pulled up for her, her elbows on the desk ledge, and watched eagerly. In the news section reporters had their pencils and pads ready on the slanting arms of their chairs. Above, both visitors' galleries were a sea of faces, with black dots of earphones in evidence. Lisa smiled as she saw the familiar seat testers and dial fiddlers already at work. The acoustics of this room were so good that you needed the earphones only for translation, but it was human nature to play with a gadget and some found it necessary to switch from French to Russian to Spanish to Chinese, though they understood no word of these languages. Simultaneous translations could be heard in the booth too, by turning a dial, but the present speaker was the compelling former president of the Philippine Islands, Carlos Romulo, and he was using English.

Lisa knew he was a brilliant speaker and writer, and she watched him with interest. Once more she felt a sense of elation that so small a nation was being given equal right to be heard with the giants and listened to so attentively.

When General Romulo's speech was concluded, Norman turned off the loud-speaker for a moment.

"Have you seen the morning papers?" he asked.

Lisa nodded wryly. "You mean the usual wails about the veto?"

"You'd think the whole United Nations must stand or fall by that alone. But whether there's a veto or not, there still has to be a majority accord and cooperation. Of course the veto use needs to be changed, but people simplify unrealistically."

Another speaker was on his feet now and they listened again. Lisa knew nothing could happen quickly and dramatically. Everyone must be heard. But now and then an argument started and the Chair had to step in. The machinery sometimes seemed ponderous, slow-moving, but the important thing was that it moved. Outside, the world watched and waited, and the men and women of press, radio, and television were its eyes and ears.

When they had been in the booth less than an hour some late arrivals came to take over, and Norman and Lisa had to give up their listening post. But Norman made no move to return to his department at once.

"Let's go outside a minute," he said, "and get some non-air-conditioned air."

They went downstairs to the lower level and out through the garden to the walk along the river front. Water that had looked gray all winter was bright blue today, and gulls soared white and silver in the sun. The two leaned on the rail and watched the birds dart toward the water in their never-ending search for food. Just as she and Reland had stood here one day last fall, Lisa thought.

Norman ceased to watch the gulls. "What has happened to you, Lisa?" he said.

"Happened?" She was puzzled.

"There's a sort of – quiet – in you that wasn't there before. Is it because your job problem is settled?"

"Perhaps," she said. "At least partly."

"You seem to have stopped the shadow-fighting that I've felt in you before."

"Have I been fighting shadows?" She looked at him quickly. He had put it well. She had been running away from the danger of being hurt. She had felt she could not risk herself and she had slapped at the shadows and fled from them. "I think Reland has taught me something about courage," she mused.

"She has taught me too," he said soberly. "That's one reason I wanted to throw you two together. I wanted you to know her better. Have you heard that Reland is going home?"

"She told me," Lisa said. "I – I thought you might ask her to stay."

"Ask her to stay?" He was plainly puzzled, but he went on to something which interested him more. "I thought I'd see you more often

309

while Reland was there. But you ran away from me. I wonder if you know how confused I've felt for the past few months. About quite a few things."

"I think I know a little," she admitted.

He looked away from her. "I've always thought I'd marry someday. But I had lofty ideas on the subject and pretty superior notions about just what sort of girl it would be safe to marry. I didn't want to make the mistake my mother made or that so many people seem to make these days. It's only lately that I've been coming around to the conviction that safety isn't everything in life. Not for nations or for men. Besides, I want a flesh and blood girl, not an image on a pedestal."

She was very still, not wanting to stop him, but not daring to be sure of where he was leading. He turned about with his back to the rail, looking up at the tall shaft of glass and steel that was the Secretariat dwarfing the pigmies at its feet. But he did not gaze at the building for long. He was looking straight into her face now.

"What am I making speeches for?" he asked, smiling at his own wordiness. "What I want to say is pretty simple, after all. I'm in love with you, Lisa. I didn't want to be – I can tell you that now. But nobody asked me, including you – yet here I am. And now I like it a lot."

She had to hold back a little, not quite daring to believe, wanting everything to be sure and out in the open.

"I'm not my mother's sort of woman," she said, looking down at her toes, "nor Reland's sort, nor Margie's, nor Arden's. I'm not always peaceful, and I suspect I want terribly to do some work outside a home. And I'm –"

"You're the girl I happen to love," Norman said, "and this isn't a very good place to kiss her, with all those Secretariat windows staring. Come inside."

He took her hand and they went together to the doors that led into the basement corridor. The door of the radio department was closed. The benches were empty. The long stretch of corridor boasted only two girls walking the other way at the far end.

He kissed her, and it was not a hard, angry kiss as it had been that other time. But it was not a very long kiss because a door behind them opened and they moved apart just in time.

"I suppose," he said, "that I'll have to get back to work. Have dinner with me tonight, Lisa? To celebrate?"

She nodded happily, somehow too choked to talk. He went toward the door of his

department and she started down the corridor
without purpose or direction. In a moment he
was back, calling after her.

"Lisa! I forgot to ask – are you going to
marry me?"

She burst out laughing because it was fun to
be silly now. But she could only nod at him
happily. He disappeared for good then and
she walked on, not quite certain of the earth
beneath her feet, lost in a dream.